Hat Trick!

Three Hockey Stories

Hat Trick!

Three Hockey Stories

Irene Punt

Cover by
Ken Steacy

Interior illustrations by
Bojan Redzic and Ken Steacy

Scholastic Canada Ltd.
Toronto New York London Auckland Sydney
Mexico City New Delhi Hong Kong Buenos Aires

Scholastic Canada Ltd.
604 King Street West, Toronto, Ontario M5V 1E1, Canada

Scholastic Inc.
557 Broadway, New York, NY 10012, USA

Scholastic Australia Pty Limited
PO Box 579, Gosford, NSW 2250, Australia

Scholastic New Zealand Limited
Private Bag 94407, Botany, Manukau 2163, New Zealand

Scholastic Children's Books
Euston House, 24 Eversholt Street, London NW1 1DB, UK

www.scholastic.ca

Library and Archives Canada Cataloguing in Publication

Punt, Irene, 1955-
[Novels. Selections]
Hat trick! : three hockey stories / Irene Punt ; illustrated by Bojan
Redzic and Ken Steacy.

Contains three previously published novels.
Contents: The wicked slapshot -- The funny faceoff -- Hockey rules.
ISBN 978-1-4431-1350-2 (softcover)

I. Redzic, Bojan, illustrator II. Steacy, Ken, illustrator III. Punt,
Irene, 1955- . Wicked slapshot. IV. Punt, Irene, 1955- . Funny faceoff.
V. Punt, Irene, 1955- . Hockey rules. VI. Title.

PS8581.U56A6 2017   jC813'.54   C2017-901494-3

7 6 5 4 3   Printed in Canada   121   19 20 21 22 23

Hat Trick!
Contents

*To my boys — Harty, Tom and Dave;
my parents; and my pals — Anne, Joanne
and Vivien. Thanks, team!*

— I. P.

Contents

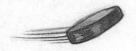

Hockey Camp

It was the hottest day of August and the first day of Champs Hockey Camp. Tom crouched on the driveway, checking his hockey bag.

"Skates, helmet, jersey, shin pads, shoulder pads, elbow pads, pants." He glanced down the street and then burrowed to the bottom of the bag — where dried-up

sports socks and used-up tape rolls lurk.

He continued, "Neck guard, mouthguard, gloves, hockey socks, sock tape, jock. Okay. Everything's here." He zipped up the bag.

The street was still empty. His friends were nowhere in sight. He picked up his lucky stick and shot a couple of tape rolls onto the lawn.

"Hurry up," said his mom, rushing toward the car. "Get your stuff in the trunk."

Tom strained to lift his bag. It felt as if it were filled with boulders. "Ugh." He dropped it down again and plunked himself on top. "It's not fair!"

"What's the matter?" asked Mom, confused. "You've been counting the days till hockey camp all summer."

Tom sighed. "Mark's on a trip with his family. Jordan's gone to goalie camp. And now

Stuart's wrecked his ankle skateboarding. I wanted to go to hockey camp with my friends. It won't be any fun without them."

"You don't need a friend at camp," said Mom. "Hockey's your friend." She gave him a pat on the back. "You'll have lots of fun. C'mon, it's *hockey*!"

Tom looked up and forced a smile as he heaved his bag into the trunk. He knew the ride to the arena was going to be lonely and boring without his friends. Together they were a team. They all loved hockey — all year round.

Mom backed out of the driveway. Tom reached over and found his favourite station on the radio. His mom turned up the volume two notches. And everything seemed a little better.

At the Arena

Bright sunlight lit up the silver letters: Centennial Arena.

Tom carried his stick over his shoulder and lugged his hockey bag through the sliding doors. Lots of information was printed on the message board in thick, black letters. Tom headed over to read it.

Everyone laughed when they read the

message. Even Tom. He walked past the

snack counter, through some doors, behind

the spectator stands, down a long hall and

into dressing room #6. He propped up his

stick against the others in the corner.

Tom scanned the room. It was crowded

WELCOME TO CHAMPS HOCKEY CAMP!

SMILE!
This place is tooooo cold for mosquitoes.

Boys go to dressing room #6.
Girls go to dressing room #3.

No fishing. No bonfires. No tenting.
This isn't just camp —

IT'S HOCKEY CAMP!

See you on the ice.
Coach Dave

and noisy and everyone seemed to know somebody. Some of the boys were wearing the same team T–shirts with Hawaiian shorts. They jostled and joked loudly, like best friends. *Where should I sit?* Tom began to worry. Relax, he told himself. But it was weird not recognizing one face. It was weird not having Stuart, Mark and Jordan with him. He let out his breath and sat down on the bench next to a boy with red hair.

"Hi," said Tom.

"Hi," said the boy, concentrating on taping his socks.

Tom started rooting through his bag, looking for his jock. He suited up quickly. By the time he was tightening his skates, everyone else was dressed and ready to go. Now the change room looked familiar. *Hockey players are hockey players*, thought Tom, seeing everyone tall in their skates

and anxious for ice. Just before he put on his helmet, he wrote his name on a piece of masking tape and stuck it on the front, above the face mask. He could feel the excitement, the nearness of hockey, as they filed out of the room. He couldn't wait to play.

Tom followed the rubber flooring to the entrance gate where the players lined up, waiting. The Zamboni made one last sweep down the middle of the ice and headed for the parking stall. The driver jumped down and closed the wide doors.

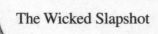
"We can go on now!" shouted one of

the kids.

Fourteen boys and four girls launched

themselves one by one onto the freshly flooded rink. Tom loved the feel of the smooth ice under his blades. He glided out and then bent down automatically to stretch his back.

BOOM! The heavy gate banged shut and was secured with a big metal latch.

Here we go, thought Tom, and a smile spread across his face.

Ninety-Nine Laps

A whistle blew. At centre ice a tall man with curly hair was waving them over.

"I'm Coach Dave. Welcome to the coolest place in town!" he announced, tipping his Calgary Flames cap.

Everyone laughed.

"Now for my icebreaker question,"

Coach Dave continued. "What was Wayne Gretzky's number?"

The red-haired boy called out, "99!" before Tom could answer.

Coach Dave had a sly look on his face. "Today is Power Skating day. In honour of The Great One, let's skate 99 laps around the rink."

"99 laps!" gasped the kids.

Tom felt as if he had swallowed a puck. He could never skate 99 laps!

"Just kidding." Coach Dave winked. "We'll start with nine. Nine fast ones. In hockey we play one goal, one period and one game at a time."

Coach Dave blew his whistle and the players took off. Tom's blades cut into the ice, and he thought, *I can easily skate nine fast laps.*

Coach Dave shouted, "Heads up! Extend your leg!"

By the third lap, Tom forgot all about missing his friends.

Coach Dave shouted, "Bend your knees! Use your arms!"

By the fourth lap, Tom forgot all about summer.

Coach Dave shouted, "Pick up the pace!"

By the fifth lap, Tom noticed the red-haired boy again. The name tag on his helmet said *Harty*. They skated neck and neck at the front of the pack for five, six, seven laps.

"Keep going!" Harty shouted.

The last two laps were the hardest. Tom was out of breath and thirsty and his leg

muscles burned. He looked at Harty. Harty's

face was red and his strides were slowing

down.

"Don't stop!" Tom shouted.

Finally, nine laps. Tom and Harty raised

their arms and cheered. "We did it!" They

coasted toward the water bottles lined up on the boards. Coach Dave flipped his stick around, and tapped the butt end twice. "Way to go!"

Tom and Harty, catching on to Coach Dave's signal, tapped their sticks, too. "Way to go!" Each picked up a water bottle and sucked back a big gulp.

Tom's heart was pounding. He tried to slow down his breathing. "Good work, Harty. You're fast."

"Yeah, good work . . . Tom." Harty smiled at him. "You're fast, too."

"Don't get too comfortable," warned Coach Dave, watching the last skater finish. He rubbed his hands together. His eyes lit up. He cleared his throat and said, "At the whistle, nine laps — backwards!" He blew the whistle loud and strong.

"Let's go," said Harty, giving Tom a nudge with his elbow.

They circled the rink together.

Tom wondered how many laps they were going to skate in one day. *What if Coach Dave makes us skate nine laps eleven times? Nah*, he thought, *Coach Dave said he was joking about 99 laps.* But was he?

At the end of the day, Tom sat on the arena steps in the hot sun, waiting for his dad. His knees hurt and his stomach growled for dinner. He hadn't felt this great all summer.

Harty stumbled out the doors carrying his hockey bag. His head was soaked with sweat. "I sure feel like I skated 99 laps today. My legs are doing the wet noodle!"

Tom burst out laughing. "Mine, too!"

"Now we're The Great Ones!" laughed Harty, slapping a high five with Tom.

It isn't bad sitting out in the sun with a new friend, thought Tom. "Hey, where do you live, anyway?" he asked.

"Out near the airport. What about you?" Harty said.

"The other way. Near the reservoir." Tom shrugged.

"We couldn't live farther apart!" exclaimed Harty.

"No kidding." Tom knew it took at least 45 minutes to get from his house to the airport.

HONK! HONK! A truck blasted its horn.

Tom looked up. "Hey, that's my dad." He grabbed his stick and bag. "I'll see you tomorrow."

"Okay, see you tomorrow," waved Harty, spotting his mom.

Away they drove in opposite directions.

A Wicked Slapshot

On Tuesday, Tom
retaped his stick
before breakfast.
He was in the car five
minutes early. "Hurry
up, Mom!" he called,
tempted to honk the horn.

Mom rushed across the driveway and jumped in the car. "Hmm," she said. "Hockey fever again?"

"Yeah," he answered, smiling. He put on his sunglasses and punched in his favourite radio station. "It's Shooting Day. And I *looooooove* to shoot the puck!"

His mom agreed. "You are always practising your shot. Sometimes I think you practise in your sleep!" She laughed.

Tom nodded his head to the music. "I do!" He closed his eyes, visualizing his shot and the puck flying into the net.

Coach Dave met the kids at centre ice with a large bucket of practice pucks. He showed them different ways to shoot the puck. Forehand. Backhand. Flip shot. Wrist shot. Snap shot. And a wicked slapshot.

"The best place to shoot is 'top shelf,'" he said. "That's at the top of the net. It's where Momma hides the cookies."

Everyone laughed.

"Okay, everybody grab a puck and spread out, facing the boards. Try at least . . ." Coach Dave raised his voice, "99 shots!"

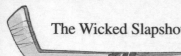

"You're on!" shouted Tom.

"I'm joking!" said Coach Dave. "Make it twenty."

Tom sighed. He would have loved to have 99 shots. He flipped a puck to Harty, then scooped one for himself.

BANG. BANG. Tom took slow, careful shots, then picked up speed. *BANG. BANG. BANG.*

The whistle blew. "Now, get a partner and listen up," said Coach Dave. "The first pair to score a hat trick on the goalie wins pucks. Not just any pucks, but pucks autographed by me!"

Tom smiled at his new friend. "C'mon, Harty! You're my partner. We're the fastest skaters here!"

Harty winced. "You won't want me for a

partner. I only got one goal last season. A hat trick is three."

"Don't worry. I read that Wayne Gretzky only got one goal in his first season of minor hockey," said Tom. He motioned to Harty, "Let's go! We can do it!"

"Okay," said Harty, sounding doubtful. He chewed on his mouth guard.

They got in line. Team after team charged down the ice, passing, passing, passing . . . THWACK! THWACK! The puck flew everywhere. It hit the spectator glass. It banged off the boards. It shot up into the stands.

And it was stopped by the goalie.

Finally it was Tom and Harty's turn. Coach Dave blew the whistle and they were off. Tom passed the puck right onto Harty's stick. Harty, striding powerfully up the outside, pulled the goalie over to the left while Tom raced up the middle. Just at the right second, Harty passed the puck over to Tom, and Tom one-timed it into the net.

"Yeah, baby!" yelled Tom, punching his gloved fist in the air.

"Woo-ooo, Tom! You've got a wicked slapshot!" shouted Harty.

"Thanks!" Tom grinned. He tapped

Harty's shoulder. "*You* set me up perfectly!"

They stood in line, watching the puck

as it slid and flew. *THWACK!* Two brothers

scored. *THWACK!* Two girls scored.

THWACK! Two big guys scored. Everyone

hollered and cheered.

The goalie widened his stance. He

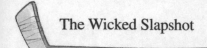

positioned his stick. He braced himself.

"We can do it," Tom assured Harty. But on their second shift Harty's shot missed the net.

On their third try, Harty passed the puck to Tom and Tom scored again with another wicked slapshot.

"Wheeee . . . eew!" Harty whistled loudly.

"Hey, we're tied for the lead!" cried Tom. "Just one more goal and we win the . . . !" Before he could finish his sentence — *SWOOSH!* A puck flew into the net and the two-girl team leapt in the air, celebrating.

Tom's jaw dropped. "What?"

"Hat trick!" shouted Coach Dave. He flipped his stick around and tapped the butt end twice. Then he waved the winners over and presented them with the two autographed pucks. They held them up proudly, with big smiles on their faces.

Everyone elsc clapped and cheered, "YAAAAY!" But as Harty applauded he kept his head down and skated to the back.

— ● —

At the end of the day, Tom and Harty sat outside on the arena steps, sucking back slush drinks in the hot sun.

"These are better than rubber pucks any day!" said Tom, holding the cold cup to his cheek.

"I guess. But I still wish I got that goal." Harty looked at Tom. "Your slapshot is so wicked. How do you do it?"

Tom could see Harty's frustration and disappointment. "Practice, I guess. That's all. Lots of practice!"

HONK! HONK! The boys looked up. Their rides were waiting.

"See you tomorrow," they said together.

"Jinx!"

They broke into laughter, slapping high fives.

Games and Goodbyes

Wednesday flew by. Coach Dave worked on skills and drills. At two o'clock, Coach Dave announced, "Let's scrimmage!"

"Yay!" Tom cheered the loudest. He had been dying for a game.

"Dark jerseys against light jerseys," Coach Dave called out.

Tom skated over to Harty. "We're on the same team!"

"No cherry-picking!" warned Coach Dave. He dropped the puck. "Look for open ice!" He headed for the boards. "Show me your best!" And everyone did.

———— ● ————

Thursday flew by. Coach Dave taught them six new plays and how to play safe. *Wow!* thought Tom. *He's a stickler for safety.*

"Keep your sticks down! Keep your heads up! Focus! Beware of the boards! An injured hockey player can't play hockey!"

Coach Dave repeated his tips loud and clear. He banged the butt end of his stick when he saw something he liked. "Good work! Yes! Fantastic! Keep it clean." He turned his Flames cap around and scrubbed the ice with his stick as though he were cleaning it. "Scrub-a-dub-dub! No penalties here!" Everyone laughed.

The words stuck in Tom's brain. "Stick down. Head up. Focus." He managed to do things right even while his brain buzzed from all the thinking, listening, watching and remembering.

Before he knew it, it was two o'clock and

Coach Dave was announcing, "Enough! Let's scrimmage!"

"Yay!" the group cheered, circling around their coach.

"Sticks in!" he said. All the kids threw their sticks into the middle. Coach Dave divided them into two piles.

Tom and Harty grabbed theirs. They

were on the same team. They raced to the bench and gulped back some water. They were ready to go.

— ● —

On Friday afternoon when the scrimmage started, Tom felt like a pro. Every skill and trick was working for him. He could play and take instructions at the same time. And he was glad he was on the same team as Harty again.

Inside the players' box, he stood by the gate, waiting for a line change. "I wish camp lasted another week!"

"Me too," said Harty, stepping onto the ice with him. Harty snatched the puck with his stick and he was off — clearly the fastest skater at camp. Just past the blue line, he wound up and took a shot on net. The shot was wide and the puck hit the boards.

"Argh!" Harty groaned.

Tom kept quiet. He wished he knew what to say.

Harty hadn't scored a goal all week. His shots were always high or wide.

At three o'clock, when Champs Hockey Camp was nearly over, Coach Dave blew his whistle and signalled for everyone to meet at centre ice for a group photograph. The players dropped to one knee, their sticks balanced on the ice.

"Say 'Stanley Cup'!" Coach Dave snapped a few quick shots. Then he spoke seriously. "You're all fine team players and I am stressing the word 'team.' There is no 'I' in team. In hockey, you win as a team and you lose as a team. Good luck next season. And have fun! Play hockey because you want to!" He flipped his stick around and tapped the butt end twice.

While everyone was banging their stick on the ice, Harty got to his feet and skated from under the bench and returned to centre ice. Everyone was smiling except the coach. He just looked puzzled.

"Thank you, Coach Dave," said Harty, trying hard not to laugh, "from all of us." He presented the coach with a thank-you gift. It was a giant tape-ball, made from everyone's old sock tape.

"Wow! Thanks," said Coach Dave, with a chuckle. "You guys will always stay . . .

er, I mean, *stick* . . . in my memory. Now, everyone on the blue line — with your right glove off."

What is Coach Dave up to now? wondered Tom, while he skated into place. When the line was complete, Coach Dave took off his own right glove and his Flames cap and skated down the line, looking each player right in the eye and shaking hand after hand. When he was done, all the players threw their gloves in the air. "Yay!" they cheered, circling around Coach Dave. "Woo hoo!"

"Now, go get your shorts on," said

Coach Dave. "It's summer out there and the mosquitoes are hungry!"

When the players reached the dressing room, a surprise was waiting for them. Coach Dave had tucked a coupon into everyone's shoe: "GOOD FOR ONE FREE SLUSH DRINK."

———●———

As Harty and Tom sat on the arena steps for the last time, watching cars pull into the parking lot, Tom got an idea. "How about sleeping over at my house tonight, if it's okay with our parents?"

"Sure!" Harty's face beamed. "I know my mom'll say yes — if she has time to drive me."

"There's my mom now!" Tom waited for her to park, and then he ran over to talk to her. She looked over at Harty and smiled.

Tom ran back to Harty, waving his arms. "You can come after dinner. And make sure you bring your hockey stick."

"My mom's here!" Harty's mom pulled into the lot and he ran to ask her.

"Yes!" he yelped, as she gave him the okay.

Their mothers got out of their cars for a chat.

"C'mon, Mom! Let's go!"

Once Harty's mom had directions to Tom's house, she looked at her watch. "Gee, I guess we should hustle. You guys live on the other side of town! Good thing I'm not working this weekend."

"See you soon!" said Harty.

"See you soon!" agreed Tom. He couldn't wait to show Harty his secret.

They drove off slurping their free slush drinks.

Practise, Practise, Practise

After dinner took forever to arrive. "Where is he?" Tom mumbled, peering down the street. He stickhandled a tennis ball up and down the driveway to pass the time.

Finally Harty's car drove up. Tom ran to greet him. They unloaded the car.

"See you tomorrow, around eleven," said Harty's mom. "Remember, you have a birthday party to go to at noon. Have fun tonight!" She waved goodbye.

"C'mon," said Tom. "Let's go." They raced to the backyard.

In Tom's backyard, giant truck tires leaned against a brick wall. An ice cream bucket filled with pucks sat on the sidewalk next to the house.

"It's target practice time!" smiled Tom, gearing into action. "This is the way I perfected my wicked slapshot." He grabbed a puck from the bucket, dropped it on the sidewalk and took a shot. "I've got some old crazy carpets, too, if you want to shoot from something slippery."

"This is awesome," said Harty. He put down his sleeping bag and reached for a puck. "I never practise at home."

"*Never?*" Tom couldn't imagine that.

"Never." Harty blushed.

The boys stood on the sidewalk, shooting puck after puck — aiming for the centres of the tires. They shot backhand and forehand. They practised all the shots Coach Dave taught them — flip shots, wrist shots, snap shots. They stood on one foot, then two. They tried some wicked slapshots.

Harty followed Tom's lead, but he didn't score. The puck always hit the wall.

"I can't believe it," sighed Harty. "What am I doing wrong?"

"I don't know," said Tom. "You look good. And you've got good power. Let's just keep shooting."

Again, they shot puck after puck, this time from the crazy carpets.

BANG! THWACK! BANG! CLUNK!

Finally, Harty got close. "Yes! That one hit the side of the tire."

"Yahoo! Keep aiming for the centre, you'll get it!" cheered Tom. But, after another hour, Harty still didn't get one in the hole.

The screen door slammed and Tom's mom carried a tray of snacks to the picnic table: watermelon, veggies, crackers, pepperoni sticks and a pitcher of lemonade. "Your arms must be falling off!" she teased. "Here, recharge your batteries."

Harty put down his stick and rummaged through his overnight bag. "I brought some snacks, too." He pulled out a couple of chocolate bars and two cans of cola. He held up the pop. "Ever tried mixing this with lemonade? My friend Jake and I call it slug slime."

"Yuck!" said Tom's mom.

"Yummm!" said Tom, mixing them each a glass. "Cheers, man."

"Cheers."

They clinked glasses. Tom swallowed a big mouthful. "Not bad," he admitted. They grabbed some pepperoni and went to collect the pucks scattered at the fence.

When they picked up their sticks again, Tom's mom had her digital camera and was taking pictures. "Now, smile, Tom. I know you're having fun."

"Mom, *pleeeeease!*" Tom made a face.

She sure knew how to bug him.

Harty cracked up.

They kept shooting and she kept taking pictures.

When it got dark, Tom's dad pulled up in his truck.

"Hi, guys!"

"Hi Dad!" said Tom.

"Hey, how about some night lights? It's pitch-black out here!" He parked the truck on the cement pad so that the headlights shone on the targets. He switched the radio to Tom's station.

"Wow!" said Harty, looking impressed. "Now this is the coolest place in town!"

"You must be Harty," said Tom's dad. "I've been hearing about hockey camp all week." He grabbed his stick from the garage and took a few shots. "Oops. That tire's a good goalie," he laughed. He dropped the last puck and took another shot. It went right into the hole.

"Now let's see your stuff," said Tom's dad, glancing at Harty.

Harty looked down, embarrassed. "I'm hopeless," he said.

"What?" said Tom's dad, shaking his head. "Tom says you're the fastest thing on skates."

"My shots are hopeless."

Tom's dad helped him with his grip and set-up. Still, Harty did not score.

— ● —

Totally exhausted, the boys spread out their sleeping bags in the back of the truck.

Just before closing his eyes, Tom said, "I knew the best thing about summer would be hockey camp."

"No kidding," said Harty. "It was a blast.

I wish we were pros and Coach Dave was our coach."

"He rocks!" said Tom.

Within minutes, they fell asleep with their NHL dreams.

Email

Breakfast came too
soon. Tom's mom
made whole wheat
pancakes with fresh

strawberries and sausage patties.

She poured some juice and turned to the

computer. "Look, you guys. You've already

got an email from Coach Dave!"

There on the screen was a photo of them all at centre ice — with a caption: Champs Hockey Champions.

"I got it, too!" said Harty, seeing his email address in the list.

"You look like a bunch of wet-heads," joked Tom's mom. "Hey, hope you two had showers last night!"

Their faces turned bright red.

Tom's mom rolled her eyes.

"We're busted," said Tom, piling up pancakes.

After they had stuffed themselves, Tom

said "Harty, let's play one-on-one street hockey till you get picked up."

They had barely started when Harty's mom pulled into the driveway. She was in a hurry. "Hi guys. Gotta go, Harty. I have to get you to this party on time. It's a movie, remember — and it's a long way back." She popped the trunk. "How was last night?"

"We practised shooting pucks," answered Harty, loading his stuff in.

"Really?" said his mom, smiling. "A whole week wasn't enough, eh?"

"Nope! We kept going till really late."

Harty hesitated for a second. "Hey, Mom —

does Grampa still have those old tires?"

"I think so." His mom looked puzzled.

"What for?"

"Thanks a ton," Harty shouted, waving

wildly as they drove away. "Bye!"

"Bye!" Tom waved back, until the car

disappeared around the corner.

— ● —

Later that day, Tom flipped through

the photos on his mom's digital camera.

Suddenly, something stood out in every

shot of Harty. "That's it!" he cried. He

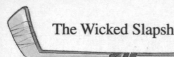

hurried to the computer and found Harty's

email address from Coach Dave's message.

He began to type.

Hi Harty,

Keep your eyes open when you shoot. And don't take them off the target. That should do the trick. Maybe a hat trick! Take a good look at the photos I'm attaching. Have fun playing hockey this wInter.

Your friend,
Tom

The phone rang. It was Mark. He was home from his trip and looking for a street hockey game.

Tom called Jordan. Jordan was ready to practise what he'd learned at goalie camp.

The doorbell rang. Stuart's ankle was better and his three cousins were in town. They all loved hockey.

Tom grabbed his stick and a tennis ball.

As they set up the nets, Tom announced, "I'm going to make you guys drink slug slime after our first period."

"What?" they screeched.

"You'll love it."

While Tom played street hockey with his friends, an email arrived in his inbox.

Hi Tom,

Thanks for the tip. I'm going to try really hard to keep my eyes open and on the target. My Grampa is setting up some tires tonight. And I'm going to practise every day I can.

Your friend,
Harty

PS Rent the movie *Wartman on Ice*. It rocks!

The Tournament

Five months went by. By the middle of January Tom's hockey team, the Glenlake Hawks, was having its best season ever. Tom loved playing centre with Mark on right wing, Stuart on defence and Jordan in goal. He loved playing anytime, anywhere — on the street, at the arenas and on the outdoor rinks.

— ● —

It was the first day of the big city tournament. Tom sat in the back seat of his dad's truck as it made its way over the snow-covered roads to Centennial Arena, lost in his own thoughts.

He took a deep breath. The closer they got to the arena, the tighter his stomach knotted. *Okay, focus*, he told himself. In his mind he could see the puck behind the net. He could see himself reach out and make the perfect wraparound shot. *Yep*. The puck whipped into the net, right past the goalie's glove.

"There's Stuart's van," said Tom's mom, interrupting his concentration. The parking lot was packed. "And . . . oh good . . . Coach Howie's car."

Tom smiled. It always felt good recognizing some cars, because it meant he was at the right arena at the right time and his friends were, too.

Tom's dad carried the bag while Tom stickhandled an invisible puck along the sidewalk and through the arena doors.

Dozens of people swarmed the entrance area. Many were bundled in bulky jackets, holding blankets and drinking hot chocolate.

Tom scanned the message board, looking for his dressing room number. He grabbed his bag and headed down the hall. Some of the kids he passed were wearing team colours he'd never seen before. Then Mark brushed by him with a slap on the back.

"Hey, Tom, I'm ready for them."

"Me too," said Jordan, a few steps behind, pulling his huge goalie bag.

"Me too," agreed Tom.

The team suited up.

Coach Howie stood in the middle of the dressing room with the league stats from the local paper. "Hawks, we are undefeated! And Jordan holds the city's shutout record!" he announced.

Everyone cheered.

"Hawks, we are rated Number One!" bellowed Coach Howie.

Everyone started chanting, "We're Number One. We're Number One."

Tom knew they were good, but he didn't know they were this good.

"Now, let's play hockey!" shouted Coach

Howie.

Hawks vs. Bulldogs

Tom's heart raced as the team filed out of the dressing room. He looked up when they reached the ice. The stands were full. He could see his grandma and grandpa. They waved.

The gates opened and the players stepped onto the ice. They skated in circles and warmed up with quick starts and stops. The clock counted down. At the whistle, the team gathered around their goalie and cheered loud and strong, "HAWKS! HAWKS! HAWKS!" Tom's line took their places on the ice while the rest of the players headed for the box.

Tom set up at centre. He looked quickly at the opposing player. His Northland Bulldogs jersey was tucked into the right side of his pants. This was exactly how Tom wore his own jersey, which was exactly how Wayne Gretzky had worn his. Tom looked at the player's face. He could see some red hair

poking out of the helmet. "Harty?" he asked.

A smile spread across his face. "Is that you?"

"Tom?" replied Harty. His smile was wider.

The ref dropped the puck. Tom took the

faceoff and raced down the ice. He passed the puck to Mark. Mark passed it back to Tom. A Bulldog blocked him. Harty grabbed the puck and shot it along the boards. Tom and Harty raced for the puck, only to be stopped by the whistle the instant Harty touched it.

"Number fifteen Northland — two minutes for tripping," shouted the ref.

A Bulldog headed for the penalty box as both coaches waved their players off the ice. The lines changed.

Tom gulped back some water, watching

the game and waiting
for his next shift. The
puck criss-crossed the
ice end to end, again
and again.

C'mon, Hawks! Tom willed a power play
goal. *C'mon! C'mon! There are only four
Bulldogs out there!*

Mark dug the puck out of the corner.
He passed it to Stuart. Stuart took a shot,
aiming for the five-hole. The Bulldogs'
goalie blocked it, rebounding the puck to
Mark. Mark took a shot. Tom looked at the

clock. Two minutes were up. A new Bulldog launched onto the ice.

Coach Howie smiled. "This is a great game. These Bulldogs are good. We can't let up. It's going to take everything we have to win this tournament."

Tom moved along the bench. He kept his eyes on #66 of the Bulldogs.

"Go Hawks, go!" Tom cheered with his team, banging his stick on the boards.

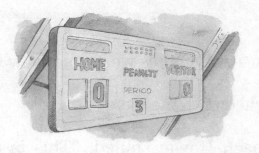

Breakaway

Near the end of the third period, the score was still 0–0.

A Bulldog iced the puck. The whistle blew. The lines changed.

Tom set up at the faceoff, facing Harty. Their eyes focused on the ice as the linesman dropped the puck. Tom won the faceoff and dropped it back to Stuart. Stuart handled the puck as though it were glued to his stick. A Bulldog player was bearing down on him so he passed the puck over to Mark. The pass was perfect, but a Bulldog winger stole the puck and passed it to Harty.

Suddenly Harty had a breakaway! He roared down the ice, his head up and his eyes on Jordan. Mark and Tom chased after him, but Harty had the jump on them. He wound up and let it fly with a wicked slapshot. The puck whizzed through the air, hitting the back of the net "top shelf" — where Momma hides the cookies.

The ref's whistle blew as he signalled.

"Goal!"

The Bulldog bench screamed and the crowd went crazy.

Tom looked at Harty, who was bending over to catch his breath. For a split second, he saw the number 66 upside-down on the back of his jersey. It looked like . . . 99!

Tom felt bad for Jordan. His shutout record was blown.

He felt bad for their defence. And with three seconds left in the game, he felt bad for his team, about to lose and be no longer "undefeated." But Tom felt good about something.

He and Harty set up for the last faceoff. As the ref held up the puck between them, Tom flipped his stick around and tapped the butt end twice.

The teams and the spectators looked puzzled.

Harty smiled at Tom. "Thanks."

The puck dropped. The clock counted

down 3 . . . 2 . . . 1 . . . *Buzzzzzzzz.*

The Bulldogs circled around Harty, cheering

and celebrating.

As the Zamboni's engine revved, the

teams skated into lines and shook hands.

When Tom and Harty met, they both flipped their sticks around and tapped the butt ends twice.

Tom's team filed back to their dressing room and slumped on the benches, still in shock.

"What was *that*?" asked Jordan.

"One wicked slapshot," said Tom. "One wicked slapshot!"

"I didn't even see it coming," sighed Jordan.

Hockey Forever

The arena steps were covered with fresh snow and the parking lot had ice thick enough to skate on. White clouds billowed from the cars as they warmed up. Tom and Harty stood side by side, downing slush drinks.

"See you tomorrow," said Harty. "Maybe both our teams will get to the finals."

"See you tomorrow," said Tom. "Now you've got a wicked slapshot!"

"Thanks!" Harty beamed. "Your pictures sure helped. I keep my eyes open now. And, boy, did I practise!"

A van pulled up with Tom's three friends in the back. Stuart called out, "Hey guys, shinny game at Chinook Park at two! See you there!"

"Want to play?" Tom asked Harty.

"Sure, I'll play 99 times a day!" he answered, tapping the butt end of his stick twice. And they both cracked up.

To Tom — for the day you sang
"Rudolph, the Red-nosed Cowboy"

— I. P.

Contents

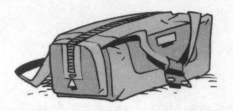

Game Time

Snow sat on top of the silver letters that spelled Centennial Arena.

Tom and Stuart lugged their big hockey bags up the stairs and through the entrance doors. They saw one of their buddies and hurried towards him.

"Hey, Mark. Wait up!"

Mark had earphones in his ears and

his brother's iPod stuck in his pocket. He turned down the music. "Wait till you guys see what I have in my hockey bag."

They made their way down the hall behind the spectator bleachers to the dressing room, where they propped up their sticks in the corner. The room was crowded.

"C'mon! C'mon!" said Tom. "Let's see!"

Mark reached into his bag. He pulled something out.

"What's that?" Tom asked.

Mark flopped down the sides and sat it upright. He took the iPod out of his pocket and placed it in the slot. "These are mini-speakers. But they make mega sound. Listen to this . . ." He turned the volume up. "My brother won some free iTunes on The Hockey Flip website."

"Cool!" said Tom.

"We are the champions of the rink . . ." Mark began to sing. He turned up the volume.

"And we make our hockey gear stink

We are the best team

We let off big steam

Toot tooty-toot toot

'Cause we are the champions of the rink!"

Everyone cracked up. Mark hit replay and the song started over. He grabbed his hockey stick and pretended it was a microphone. He sang so loud, his face turned purple.

Everyone stood, cheering and laughing. Everyone . . . except Jordan, the goalie. He was concentrating on lacing his chest pads and tightening the buckles near his ankles. Then he moved into his pre-game stretches.

"I'm trying for a new shutout record," Jordan whispered to Tom. "I gotta focus." He practised his ugly goalie face.

Tom hoped Jordan got his wish.

The door opened and in walked Coach Howie. He was waving the game sheet and carrying a case of water bottles. Tom liked Coach Howie. He was nice and he was fun.

He worked at the Smokin' Cola Company.

Sometimes he gave them free drinks after a

game.

"Okay, you hot dogs," Coach Howie said

loudly. A hockey glove flew through the

air. Coach Howie blew his whistle. "Settle

down. You're Glenlake Hawks, not loony

birds. Get your gear on. We've got a game to win!"

Tom pulled on his jersey and began taping his socks, still humming Mark's funny song.

"Which line plays first shift?" asked Stuart.

Coach Howie checked his notes. "I've got Tom at centre; Mark's right wing, Spencer's left wing, and Stuart and Ben are on defence. Jordan's in goal."

Yes! Tom cheered to himself. He looked at his friends. They were all smiling because they all got to play first shift. *We ARE the champions of the rink!* he thought.

Then Stuart caught his finger in the zipper of his hockey bag, Mark pulled on his lucky socks, and Jordan began to hiccup. It was game time.

Go, Hawks, Go!

The team filed out of the dressing room.

Tom looked up into the stands. His mom

and dad were sitting with Stuart's and

Mark's parents. They wore the team colours:

yellow and green. Tom's stomach knotted.

Why did he get so nervous before a game

anyway?

The Zamboni swept and flooded the ice, then headed for the parking stall. Coach Howie opened the gate. He took slippery steps across the ice. "Stretch and skate!" he hollered at the Hawks. "Get warmed up." He put the water bottles on the players' home bench. Then he shook hands with the ref.

Tom placed the blade of his stick on the ice. He took long, slow strides, then picked up speed. Suddenly, his head filled with,

"We are the champions of the rink

And we make our hockey gear stink

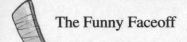

We are the best team

We let off big steam . . ."

Mark skated ahead of him, singing the same song.

"Toot tooty-toot toot!" Tom called to him.

Mark bent forward and twisted. *"Toot tooty-toot toot!"*

"Nice stretches," said Coach Howie, cheering them on.

Tom cracked up. The coach had made a joke without knowing it. Tom forgot all about being nervous.

The clock dropped to zero. The buzzer

sounded. The Hawks circled around Jordan.

"Hawks! Hawks! Hawks!" they cheered. Then

the first shift took their starting positions.

Tom set up at centre, his eyes glued to

the ice.

The ref dropped the puck and Tom

stabbed at it with his stick. The puck flew to Mark. Mark dug in his skate blades and raced up the ice with the puck. He passed it to Tom right before the blue line. Tom wound up and took a slapshot. The Sunridge Sharks' goalie stopped the puck with his blocker, but it rebounded back to Tom. Quickly he fired the puck into the net, hitting the crossbar with a *PING!*

"Wow!" cheered Mark and Stuart. They punched Tom on the shoulder. "Great goal!"

The crowd cheered.

The Hawks banged their sticks.

Tom felt great.

"We ARE the champions of the rink!" Mark sang, heading for the bench. Coach Howie held the gate open for them and the next line set up at centre ice.

The song started in Tom's head again and wouldn't quit. Calling themselves champions made him feel more sure and powerful.

"Go, Hawks, go!" cheered the fans.

"Go, Hawks, go!" cheered the players on the bench.

Three periods flew by.

The final score was 4–0 for the Hawks.

Tom headed for the dressing room. He threw his stick in the corner and whipped off his number 15 jersey. He waved it in circles over his head. "Woo hoo!" he shouted.

"Another shutout for Jordan!" announced Mark, both arms in the air. "Another two goals for Tom!" He pressed the power button on the iPod.

"We are the champions of the rink

And we make our hockey gear stink . . ."

Everyone sang, swaying in time with the music. Everyone . . . including Jordan.

"Listen up!" shouted Coach Howie. Everyone sat. "Good game, boys. You guys really burned it up out there! For a special treat, I brought you some of the new Rowdy Root Beer we're bottling at the Smokin'

Cola Company. Next game is tomorrow at 6:30." He sat down and unlaced his skates as the boys made a beeline for the drinks.

Mark began to sing, making the word "Rowdy" extra loud.

"Ninety-nine Rowdy root beers

on the wall

Ninety-nine Rowdy root beers

If one of those bottles

should happen to fall

There'll be ninety-eight Rowdy

root beers on the wall."

Tom put the open root beer bottle to his

lips. Little bubbles fizzled and jumped onto his tongue. He took a big gulp. The fizzles went down his throat and up his nose. He blinked. He pinched his nose. "Did ya feel that fizz?" he asked, eyes watering.

"Man, this root beer has gas!" said Mark, rolling his eyes.

The dressing room exploded with laughter.

"You boys are too much!" said Coach Howie, smiling.

"*You're* too much!" the team shouted back. "Thanks for the Rowdy Root Beer, Coach!"

Mark circled the dressing room in his red long underwear, collecting the empty bottles. Stuart searched for his Band-Aids. And the song went on and on and on . . .

"Eighty-three Rowdy root beers

  on the wall

Eighty-three Rowdy root beers

If one of those bottles

should happen to fall

There'll be eighty-two Rowdy

root beers on the wall.

Eighty-two . . ."

Journal Writing

Tom sat at his desk, his journal open. On the way to school he'd thought about what he might write for today. He had lots to say about last night's game. And lots to say about the game tonight. *What should I write first?* he wondered. He glanced at Jordan. Jordan was slowly sharpening his hockey pencil. He looked upset.

"*Psst*," said Stuart from behind. "Look what I put in my journal." Stuart had stuck an old Band-Aid on the page.

"That's sick," Mark said.

Tom laughed to himself at his friends. They made everything fun. Mark was always cracking jokes. Stuart was smart, but he was accident-prone.

Mrs. Wong, their teacher, walked up and down the aisles, watching them write. She stopped next to

Stuart. Tom snickered, wondering what she would say about the Band-Aid.

Mrs. Wong said, "Ouch! Stuart did a journ-*ail* entry. Get it? 'Ail' means sick." Sometimes Mrs. Wong was funny, too. It was like you could say anything to her and it was okay. Then she cleared her throat. "Now, if you're having trouble thinking of something to write, just think about what makes you happy or sad. And don't worry about your spelling. This is your journal. It should make you feel good."

Tom put his pencil to the page. For a

moment it was stuck. Then he wrote:

I play centre for the Glenlake Hawks.

We had a game last night and we won.

My first goal was a slapshot. My second

goal was a wraparound. AND!!! I almost

got a HAT TRICK — that's three goals!

Can we win tonight? Yes, WE CAN!

We have a new team song.

At the bottom of the page, Tom drew the
scoreboard: 4–0. Mrs. Wong was right. Tom
did feel good, writing about hockey and
winning — and scoring goals. He drew fire-
works around the score.

Mrs. Wong looked at Jordan. Jordan blushed. When he was in net, wearing his goalie equipment, he looked big and fearless. He could outplay the toughest teams. But when it came to school, he got anxious about some things. Writing and speaking were the worst. His journal was

blank today and nothing had been written yesterday either.

Mrs. Wong sighed. "Hmm. If that page stays blank, you'll have to stay in at recess, Jordan."

Tom knew Jordan was embarrassed. He looked around at his other friends. They had a hockey game planned for recess and they needed Jordan.

Mrs. Wong kept circling the classroom. She looked at Amber's work and cooed, "Ooooooh . . . your little white puppy looks sooooo cute."

Jill had already written two pages. "Good work, Jill!" Mrs. Wong said, taking the pencil off her ear. She drew a star on Jill's page.

Kylie's hand waved in the air. "I wrote about my Irish dancing. I went to a feis last weekend. That's a dance competition. I wrote about my dress and my music and the big trophy I won."

Mrs. Wong patted Kylie on the shoulder, "It's very nice to be excited about your life, isn't it?" She looked over at Jordan's empty page with a frown. "Better get writing. Remember, a journal entry can be one word or one hundred words. Just be yourself."

Tom thought of something weird while Mrs. Wong spoke. Jordan was being himself; worried and nervous about writing. His blank pages showed that.

Mrs. Wong said, "Maybe you should write about something you're looking forward to."

Tom tried to get Jordan's attention. "Jordan! Jordan!" he whispered, pointing to his Flames jersey. "Write about hockey! That's easy."

Kylie rolled her eyes. "Hockey, hockey, hockey."

Jordan blushed.

Tom blew out a

frustrated breath.

"Pretend your

page is a new sheet of ice that's just been

flooded. Carve it up!"

Jordan shrugged. "Okay, okay," he said.

"I am looking forward to . . ." Carefully he

drew the brown root beer bottle from Coach

Howie. Then he wrote: **ROWDY**.

Stuart howled when he saw Jordan's page.

"That's a journ-*ale* entry! Get it? 'Ale' is beer."

Tom made a face.

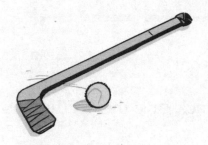

Stay Off
the Field

The recess bell rang. Tom, Mark, Stuart and Jordan put on their boots and jackets and headed for the caretaker's room.

"Hey, Mr. Mack!" chimed the boys, grabbing the floor hockey sticks from a box.

"Hey, boys!" said Mr. Mack. "How was last night's game?"

"We won!"

Mr. Mack gave them a thumbs-up. "Right on! Now, stay off the field this recess. The entire west side of the school is pure ice."

They headed for the playground. The school cast a black shadow over the field.

"Oh, man," said Stuart, watching his step. "Mr. Mack's right. Yesterday's chinook must've melted the snow into a pond and then it froze solid last night. You could break your leg out there."

"Let's go to the hopscotch area. Nobody ever uses it," suggested Tom. But when they got there, Kylie and her friends had staked

it out.

Tom took a tennis ball out of his pocket

and dropped it at his feet. He stickhandled

it around the girls. Mark clapped sticks with

him, stealing the ball.

"Over here!" said Stuart. "Pass it."

"What are you guys doing?" hissed Kylie. "We were here first. And this is where we play *Canadian Idol*. Right now, I'm dancing for my friends. And singing. And you're in our way."

Mark stopped. "Singing? We know a good song!" He winked at Tom, Stuart and Jordan. "Let's sing our face off. Get it? Faceoff!"

"What?" said Jordan.

"Yeah," whispered Mark. "Our special song."

The boys lined up in a row. They held their hockey sticks like microphones.

"One, two, three . . ." counted Mark.

"We are the champions of the rink

And we make our hockey gear stink

We are the best team

We let off big steam . . ."

The boys cracked up. *"Toot tooty-toot*

toot!"

The girls giggled. *"Toot toot!"*

Kylie scoffed, "That's an old song from The Flipflops. I know all their songs. I even bought their new CD at the book fair." She cleared her throat and sang, *"Rudolph, the red-nosed pirate . . ."*

Jill stopped Kylie. "Wait! Let's do it together."

"We need their hockey sticks," Amber announced.

Copying the boys, the girls held the sticks and sang,

"Rudolph, the red-nosed pirate,

He had only one good eye,

And if you ever saw him,

You would run away — and die!

Bye-bye!"

They dropped the hockey sticks and waved bye-bye.

Mark clutched his throat and began coughing. "I'm dying, I'm dying. I saw Rudolph, the red-nosed pirate!" he moaned with a raspy voice. "I'm *dying* — to play hockey!" He winked at his friends.

"Woo hoo!" The boys picked up their sticks and banged them on the cement.

"Wow! I've got an idea!" Kylie shrieked. "Let's ask Mrs. Wong if we can put on a show!"

"I don't want to put on a show," said Jordan. "I hate getting up at the front of the classroom. And I don't do music. I play hockey."

"It wouldn't have to be just music, Kylie," said Amber. "Let's make it . . ."

Tom tried to ignore them. He agreed with Jordan. "Let's just play hockey! This is really annoying. Recess is nearly over!"

Mark reached for the tennis ball. He stickhandled it toward Jordan, then passed it to Tom. Jordan moved into a crouch. Tom fired a shot. Jordan hit the ball, sending it flying toward the field. Stuart ran after it. The instant he set foot on the ice he slipped and fell, scraping his hand raw.

"I need that Band-Aid from my journal," he moaned.

BUZZZZZZZ! sounded the bell. The ball rolled to a stop on the ice.

"Everyone inside!" yelled the teacher on recess duty. "Stay off the field."

Tom threw his arms in the air. "Now we don't even have a tennis ball."

Five minutes before the end-of-day bell, Mrs. Wong said, "I've got an idea." She picked up a piece of chalk and wrote on the board:

JOURNAL SHOW AND TELL TOMORROW

"What?" yelped Mark.

"I know, I know. Some of the girls have asked to show off their work. I think it's wonderful to be excited about writing. Keep in mind you can choose whatever you want to tell the class about."

"I'm writing ten more pages about Irish dancing," said Kylie, smiling.

"And I'm bringing props for the show!" said Amber.

"Show?" said Stuart.

"*Show* and Tell!" said Jill. "I'm bringing a tuba."

"Props are not necessary, but they would be nice," said Mrs. Wong. "Just make sure your presentation is only a few minutes."

"Maybe some parents can make cookies," suggested Amber.

"Yum!" Mrs. Wong smiled. "This is going to be fun!"

Tom sunk down in his desk. He liked to get good marks at school and make Mrs. Wong happy. But tonight he didn't have time to do math homework, get extra things like props together and ask his mom to make cookies. He had a hockey game at 6:30!

Tom flipped through his journal. Quickly, he drew a big unhappy face on the last page. Inside a speech bubble he wrote,

ARGGHHH!

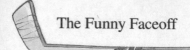

For some reason, looking at this page made him feel much better.

Goalie Action

It was seven o'clock. Westside Arena was freezing. The ref blew his whistle as he raised his arm. "Icing!" The players skated back toward the far faceoff circle, near the Hawks net. As Tom glided across the ice, he glanced at the scoreboard and time clock. It was already second period. The Glenlake Hawks were winning 1–0 against

the Westhill Wolves. But they'd just made

a big mistake. And now the Wolves had a

chance to score.

Coach Howie stood in the players' box.

He had one hand on the gate, one hand on

the latch. "Tom! Stuart! Off!" he hollered.

They hustled off the ice; Mark and

Spencer launched on.

"Cool it on the hot-dog moves!" said

Coach Howie. "No one-man shows out there. We play as a team. Pass the puck. Keep the Wolves guessing. Do your best."

The linesman dropped the puck. The Wolves' number 13 won the faceoff, passing it to his winger. He fired the puck onto the boards. It ricocheted. Their winger knocked the flying puck down with his glove and picked it up on his stick. He took three giant strides and fired the puck at the net. *DONK!* The puck hit Jordan's goalie stick. It rebounded and number 13 was there. *BANG!* He shot the puck again. Jordan's stick deflected it again. Again number 13 got the rebound. *SHWOOP*. The puck slid and Jordan flew full-stretch, landing on the ice and covering the puck.

The crowd went crazy, screaming and whistling.

The Hawks bench went nuts. "Holy moley, what a goalie!" they yelled, banging their sticks on the boards. Jordan had saved them again.

The linesman grabbed the puck from Jordan and skated to the faceoff circle.

Tom gulped. "Did you see that winger?"

he asked Stuart. "And number 13 is bad luck — well, for us."

"Did you see Jordan?" gasped Stuart. "He stopped every shot . . . but can he keep it up?"

Tom and Stuart looked at each other with the same nervous face. "I sure hope so!" they said at the same time.

— ● —

Thirty minutes later, the Hawks were in the dressing room, dancing.

"We are the champions of the rink

And we make our hockey gear stink

We are the best team

We let off big steam . . ."

"Great game!" cheered Coach Howie. "3–0. ANOTHER shutout for Jordan! But — too many penalties."

Everyone looked at Mark. "Goon!"

"Oops!" he said. And the look on his face said, "Sorry."

Coach Howie opened his hockey bag. Two dozen Rowdy Root Beer bottles sat inside. "Help yourselves!" he said, smiling. "I thought you *smokin'* hot players might need to cool off!"

Everyone laughed. Sometimes Coach

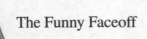

Howie was really funny.

Tom, Mark and Stuart opened their bottles.

"*Rowdy!*" said Mark.

They gulped the root beer back.

Jordan put his bottle in his hockey bag, next to the root beer from the day before. "I'm saving mine," he whispered to Tom. "I can never have anything right after a game, until my nerves settle down."

"Hey, I got my prop for tomorrow's journal thing," Stuart announced, pulling off his hockey glove. He showed everyone his bruised hand with a large Band-Aid on top. The bruise and the Band-Aid were purple, red and green.

"Props!" moaned Mark. "What's with *that*?"

Jordan slouched on the bench, looking miserable. "I don't know what I'm going to do when Mrs. Wong makes me read something from my journal. I always get the hiccups when I'm nervous. And you know what else . . ."

Tom knew. Jordan stuttered if he was super nervous, and he didn't want anyone to notice. Sometimes he stuttered before an important game. But it always went away once he was between the pipes.

Jordan slumped against the wall. The black cage of his helmet dropped down over his face. Suddenly he looked fierce.

Tom had an idea. "I wrote

about hockey in my journal. I could bring my Hawks jersey to school for my prop." He shook Jordan's shoulders. "Why don't you wear all your goalie stuff? You could show everyone the mean goalie face you make. And you could show an empty page in your journal and say, 'This is how many pucks got by me this season!'"

Jordan brightened. He thought for a few seconds. "Will I look like a weirdo totally suited up?"

"I'll wear all my equipment, too," said Stuart.

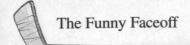
"Me, three," nodded Mark.

"C'mon, Jordan." Tom kept trying. He held his fist out and the boys banged their fists on top.

"*Hawks!*" they cheered.

Jordan smiled. "You're right. I'm never nervous on the ice, once the game starts. I only get pre-game jitters. Maybe I'll get a shutout at school with my equipment on."

"Make it a *shout*-out!" said Mark. "Get it? Speak up good and loud!"

Everyone groaned.

Journal Show and Tell

During lunch hour the next day Tom and Jordan got dressed in the boys' washroom.

"I'm so n-n-nervous," said Jordan. "I'm a l-l-loser."

"You are not. And you'll be great. Just think about our song when you're standing at the front. *We are the champions of the rink!* It'll make you feel strong." Tom smiled. He liked how it felt when he called himself a champion. "C'mon!" He nudged Jordan and together they sang, *"We are the champions of the rink!"*

On the way down the hall, they saw Mr. Mack in the caretaker's room.

"How's it going?" he asked.

"We are the champions of the rink!" Tom cheered.

"Good going!"

— ● —

Everyone was scurrying around the classroom, getting ready for the Journal Show and Tell. Amber's mom walked in with a large platter of chocolate cookies. Amber was carrying a shiny gold bag. Out of the top poked the head of her fluffy white dog, Pickles.

Tom, Stuart and Mark huddled together in a corner of the room, wearing their hockey equipment and jerseys. "Hawks, Hawks, Hawks!" they cheered.

"Hockey, hockey, hockey," said Amber, rolling her eyes.

Jordan's huge goalie pads, gloves and blocker made him look like a giant. He squished himself into his desk, hiccupping so hard his head jolted.

Tom knew Jordan was getting nervous again. "Champion, champion," he mouthed, and winked.

Jordan hiccupped and stuttered, "Th-th-thanks."

Tom looked around the room. *Where's Kylie?* Her desk was empty. *She's the one who wanted to share journals and she's not even here!* Then the weirdest thing happened. Tom heard her voice coming from someone else in the doorway.

"Sorry I'm a bit late, Mrs. Wong. It just takes so long to get my wig on perfectly."

"Oh . . . oh, Kylie!" cried Mrs. Wong, surprised. "I barely recognized you. Your dress is lovely."

Kylie wore a shiny
orange and sapphire-
blue dress with tiny
fake diamonds sewn
all over it. It had fancy
sleeves and the skirt
looked like a huge,
open umbrella. Her
curly wig was as fluffy

and white as Amber's dog, Pickles.

When Pickles saw Kylie he went
crazy, barking and growling at her wig.
"Grrrrrrrrrrrrrrrr."

"Hush, Pickles." Amber carried him to the back of the classroom so Kylie could sit down.

Mrs. Wong clapped her hands. "People! People! I'm so pleased with this excitement, I could sing. Now, settle down and let's begin."

When everyone was ready, she announced, "I'm going to choose a name." She reached into a box on her desk and pulled out a slip of paper.

"Jill. You go first. Remember, keep it short!"

Jill walked to the front of the classroom,

carrying a strange-shaped black case. She unsnapped the clasps and pulled out a large tuba.

From her journal she read:

My grandpa's tuba was in our basement.

My mom said I was too little to play it,

but I snuck downstairs and tried anyway.

I washed the mouthpiece because

Grandpa used to spit

when he played it.

Jill sucked in a gulp of air, puffing out her cheeks like a blowfish.

She blew out, *"TOOOOOOOT!"* The tuba sounded like a whoopee cushion.

"We could use that tuba for our song," whispered Mark, grinning. *"Tooty-toot toot!"*

By two o'clock, more than half the class had shared their journal writing.

Tom looked at his friends. They were all shifting around in their seats, boiling hot. Jordan looked ill. "When's recess?" hissed Mark.

"Soon!" Tom gave him two thumbs up.

Mrs. Wong called out another name. "Kylie."

Kylie's wig and skirt bounced to the front of the classroom. "Yes! It's my turn!" She curtsied and positioned her shiny black shoes. Looking out at her classmates, she began:

Chapter One. Page one of fourteen. I am the best Irish dancer. I have won lots of trophies. I love my costume, my makeup and my wig. I want to get fake eyelashes for my birthday. I want to try out for *Canadian Idol.* I was only four years old when I got my . . .

"Lovely," said Mrs. Wong. "Unfortunately, we must limit our journal-sharing to one paragraph today."

Kylie frowned as she turned on her music. She began to step and kick and step and kick to an Irish reel. Faster and faster . . . until the end of the tune.

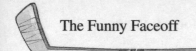

Amber's mother blurted out, "Bravo! Bravo! You students are so gifted. This is a wonderful talent show."

Mrs. Wong read the next name. "Jordan."

Rowdy

Tom, Stuart and Mark all held their breath, watching Jordan pull his goalie bag to the front of the classroom.

"Uh . . ." Jordan froze. He hiccupped. He stuttered, "Uh . . . I-I-I . . ."

Tom waved his arms, trying to get Jordan's attention. "Your helmet!" he coached. "The cage!" He began to hum, "*We are the champions of the rink . . ."*

Jordan got his helmet out of the bag, pulled it on and fastened the cage. He let out one last hiccup. Some students snickered. Instantly, Jordan wore his ugly goalie face.

"I am the goalie for the Glenlake Hawks," said Jordan in a loud voice. "I love hockey."

Mrs. Wong smiled and nodded.

"My props for today are . . ." Jordan looked out at the classroom. Froze for a second. Shook his head. He continued, "My props for today are . . . Tom, Mark and Stuart. They're on the Glenlake Hawks, too. I do best when I'm with my team."

A tingle went up Tom's spine. Jordan was FANTASTIC!

The three friends walked to the front of the classroom and stood with their goalie.

"You must read from your journal now, Jordan," said Mrs. Wong. He had never said this much at the front of the classroom. He had never said this much all year. Mrs. Wong looked proud of him.

Jordan opened his journal. He showed the picture he had drawn of the brown root beer bottle. "ROWDY!" he boomed, reading the one word on the page. Then he reached inside his equipment bag and pulled out two Rowdy bottles from the Smokin' Cola Company.

"Huh?" Everyone stood up to see.

Jordan pretended to drink.

"Journal journ-*ale!*" announced Mark.

Stuart said, "*Smokin'!* And full of gas!"

They began to laugh. Then snort. Tom tried to control himself, but he couldn't. Tears were streaming down his cheeks. He held onto his stomach to help with the shooting pains.

"Oh, man," said Mark. "I might laugh my face off. Get it? Faceoff!"

Jordan began to sing, *"Ninety-nine Rowdy . . ."*

Before another word was sung, Amber's mother plunked down the platter of cookies and stormed out of the classroom.

Inappropriate

The boys continued singing,

. . . root beers on the wall

Ninety-nine Rowdy root beers

If one of those bottles

should happen to fall

There'll be ninety-eight Rowdy

root beers on the wall."

Mrs. Wong cleared her throat. "Ahem. That song is from an old camp song. Now for the next student to share . . ." She put her hand into the box filled with names.

Knock, knock. Dr. Dean, the school principal, was standing in the doorway. "I'd like to see these boys now, please — Jordan, Mark, Stuart and Tom. Thank you."

— ● —

The boys sat down in a row on the chairs inside Dr. Dean's office. Tom's face felt hot. His heart was beating fast. He'd never been inside the principal's office before and she was not smiling.

"Can you boys guess why I've called you into my office this afternoon?" Dr. Dean was serious.

The boys looked at each other, puzzled.

"Come on," said Dr. Dean. "Think about your actions."

"Is it for going on the frozen field?" asked Stuart, showing his bruised hand and scab.

"No." Dr. Dean wrote notes. "But that is another reason to speak with you. The field is closed — and you are to keep off."

"Were we late after lunch?" asked Tom, remembering how they had said hello to Mr. Mack.

Dr. Dean wrote another note. Then she said, "I've just received a parent complaint about your choice of songs and props for a class presentation. We don't have inappropriate songs sung at our school.

Perhaps you learned this one in your hockey dressing room. And singing it at school could be cause for suspension."

Tom felt like he'd been hit in the stomach with a puck. "Does suspension mean what it means in hockey?" he asked Dr. Dean. "In hockey, you miss the next game."

Dr. Dean nodded. "In school you miss the next DAY."

Tom glanced at his friends. They all looked confused and sick.

"I didn't know we couldn't sing that," squeaked Mark. "I've heard something like it sung on the school bus."

Dr. Dean wrote more notes.

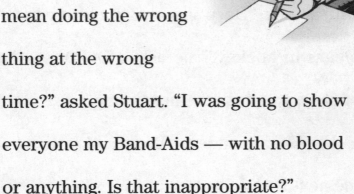

"Does 'inappropriate' mean doing the wrong thing at the wrong time?" asked Stuart. "I was going to show everyone my Band-Aids — with no blood or anything. Is that inappropriate?"

Tom took a deep breath. *What would his parents say?* To hold back his tears, he told himself over and over, *Champions. We are the champions.* But he didn't feel like one at all.

Jordan cleared his throat. "Um . . . um . . . We're here . . . be-be-because I read my j-j-journal," he stuttered. "And be-be-be-cause . . ." He hiccupped and his face went bright red.

Dr. Dean tapped her pencil.

Then Jordan dropped the cage down on his mask and said firmly, "We were told we could bring props for when we shared our journal. I wrote about Rowdy *root* beer, so I showed everyone the bottles I had. It's a new drink. Then we sang 'Ninety-Nine Rowdy Root Beers on the Wall.' We only started laughing because we were nervous."

He paused. "Everyone thinks hockey players

don't get nervous, but I do."

"Me, too," said Tom. "I get nervous."

"Oh," said Dr. Dean. Her lips twitched.

Her forehead scrunched. "Ninety-nine

bottles of *root* beer! That's a bit different

from the message I got. Jordan, you've done

a good job of explaining your side of the

story. You speak very well."

Jordan smiled as he lifted the cage of his

goalie helmet.

Tom began to wonder. How did Dr. Dean

get everything so mixed up? What did she

think they sang?

KNOCK, KNOCK,

KNOCK!

Three loud raps

on Dr. Dean's door interrupted them. "Dr.

Dean," said Mr. Mack. "We have a problem

on the field."

"What is it?" Dr. Dean asked.

"Amber took Pickles outside for recess,

and the dog ran right to the middle of the

field," explained Mr. Mack. "He saw a tennis

ball."

Dr. Dean stared. Tom gulped. It was his tennis ball.

Mr. Mack continued, "Pickles won't move and nobody can walk on the ice. What should we do?"

"Oh, dear," said Dr. Dean. "Dogs are not allowed on the field. Ever. It's a city bylaw!" She sharpened her pencil.

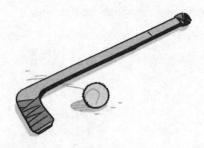

The Funny Faceoff

"Pickles! Picky!" screamed Amber. "Come here, Picky!"

Mrs. Wong, Amber's mother and the students were lined up at the edge of the field, all eyes on the little dog. Tom, Stuart, Mark and Jordan hurried toward them, with Mr. Mack and Dr. Dean not far behind.

"*Arr-ooo. Arr-ooo*," whined Pickles

weakly.

"He's scared. And he might freeze,"

sobbed Amber. "I have to rescue him." She

took one step onto the ice. *Swoosh!* She
wiped out.

Mr. Mack slid to Amber's side and lifted
her up by the elbow. *Boom!* They both fell.

"*Ouch!*" yelped Mr. Mack, rubbing his elbow. "Close call. I could have cracked my head open on this ice. *Nobody* can walk on this field until the ice melts."

"It might not melt for a *week!*" exclaimed Amber. "Pickles will *starve.*"

The class stared out across the field. Mrs. Wong tightened her scarf and pulled down her hat. She blew into her mitts. "Hmm. This is a problem."

"A big problem," agreed Dr. Dean.

Jordan said, "I'm not afraid of thick, hard ice." He knocked on his goalie helmet.

"Me, neither," said Tom.
"Our hockey equipment is
made for it." He studied
Pickles. Pickles had the

tennis ball in his mouth. Tom had an idea.
"We just need our sticks!"

"I'll be right back," said Mr. Mack, catching
on. While Mrs. Wong's class shivered at the
edge of the field, he hurried to get their
sticks from the classroom. By the time he
returned, Tom, Jordan, Stuart and Mark
had tightened their boots and helmets. They
took their sticks and looked at Dr. Dean.

"Well . . . I guess we can allow you hockey players to go onto the ice," she said.

"Be careful!" warned Mrs. Wong, as Stuart and Mark headed toward the stranded dog.

"Please save Pickles," begged Amber. *"Pleeeease!"*

"Here, Pickles," called Stuart. "Come here, Pickles."

Pickles cocked his head, then danced for the boys in the middle of the field. Stuart and Mark moved in quickly. Like wingers, they spread out around the dog. Suddenly, Pickles started to run toward busy Elbow Drive.

"The cars! The cars!" shouted Mark, running and sliding as fast as he could. "Pickles has a breakaway with the ball!" Mark fell face down. He picked himself up.

"Pickles!" snapped Stuart. "Sit! You sit!" Stuart fell backward.

Pickles stopped and turned. He wagged his tail. The look in his eyes said, "Na na na na. You can't catch me!"

"Stuart! Mark! Go the other direction!" Tom hollered. "Circle back toward the school. Pickles thinks we're playing a game with him. We have to outfox him."

Stuart and Mark turned, following Tom's suggestion. Pickles chased after them — away from Elbow Drive.

"Go, Hawks, go!" shouted the students.

There was more to do — and fast. Tom looked at Kylie. "Can I borrow your wig?" Kylie made a face, but then she took it off and handed it to Tom.

Then he and Jordan headed out on the ice.

Tom called, "Pickles! Picky, Picky, Pickles!" He shook the curly, white wig. "Come here, Pickles. I have a little dog for you to meet." Tom barked like a yappy dog.

Pickles looked at him and at the wig. Tom barked again and then dropped the wig on the ice. He stepped back. "Set up for a faceoff!" he shouted to Stuart and Mark.

Tom kept his stick on the ice, ready for Pickles. The dog pranced toward the wig,

the tennis ball still in his mouth. Then he dropped the ball to sniff the wig. Tom's plan had worked! Quickly he grabbed the tennis ball with his stick and passed it to Stuart.

"Arf! Arf!" barked Pickles, charging after the ball.

"Go, Hawks, go!" shouted the students standing on the edge of the field, watching Pickles go against the Hawks.

Stuart took a shot, firing the ball toward Jordan. Pickles bolted after the flying ball. It landed. It bounced. Jordan kept a solid goalie stance as Pickles slid across the ice. Then Jordan flew full-stretch, landing on the ice — and covering Pickles.

The students went crazy, screaming and whistling. "Yaay!" they yelled. Jordan had the dog.

"*Aarrrrr-ooooo,*" Pickles howled.

Tom, Stuart and Mark circled around Jordan and his captive. As they walked carefully off the icy field, they sang,

"We are the champions of the rink

And we make our hockey gear stink

We are the best team

We let off big steam . . ."

Jordan handed Pickles to Amber. Amber gushed, "Thank you, thank you, *thank you*!"

Tom felt proud. He looked at everyone's happy face. Then he noticed Dr. Dean shaking her head. Tom gulped. *Is Dr. Dean*

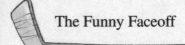

shaking her head in a good way or a bad way? It was hard to tell.

"Do you think we're in the doghouse?" asked Mark.

Finally, Dr. Dean spoke. "Well done."

Champions
of the Rink

Back in the classroom, Mrs. Wong held the box of names for Journal Show and Tell. She pulled out a name. "Tom. It's your turn."

Tom walked to the front of the class-room, carrying his journal. He opened it and began looking for something to read.

"Nope. Nope," he mumbled. Every journal entry he had made was about hockey. And now he wasn't sure what was good to read in school, and what wasn't.

"Please, Tom," said Mrs. Wong. "I'd like to hear from everyone this afternoon, if possible."

Tom looked up. "Can Mark, Stuart and Jordan be *my* props?" He winced.

"Oh, boy," said Mrs. Wong. She took a deep breath. "Okay."

Mark, Stuart and Jordan filed up and stood beside Tom. He pointed to the journal entry he'd done about their funny hockey song. "Let's sing this one," he whispered.

"Are you *crazy*?" asked Stuart.

"But I have a good idea." Tom looked at Mrs. Wong. "We need a thirty-second time out for a team meeting!"

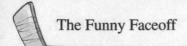

Mrs. Wong nodded.

Tom whispered something to his friends. Then they stood in a line. They positioned their wet feet. They bowed, and began to sing:

"We are the champions of the rink

And we make our hockey gear . . ."

They paused. The girls shouted out, "Stink!" And Jill got ready to toot her tuba.

Mrs. Wong raised her eyebrows. She shook her head at the girls.

The boys started over.

"We are the champions of the rink

And we make our hockey gear . . .

THINK!

We are the champions

We work together

Good friends forever

'Cause we are the champions of the rink!"

They bowed again. "THE END!" they shouted, pumping their fists in the air.

"What?" said Kylie. "That's not right. The song doesn't go like that. You missed the best part — with the toots."

Kylie got one of Mrs. Wong's looks as the boys returned to their desks.

Mrs. Wong clapped enthusiastically. "Today, you Hawks were champions on ice, rescuing Pickles. It was just like a hockey rink out there!"

"Yay, Hawks!" everyone cheered.

Four Hawks smiled from their seats.

Today was weird, Tom thought. *First, we did the wrong thing at the wrong time — according to Amber's mom. Then Dr. Dean got the wrong thing wrong. Then we did the wrong thing at the right time — by going onto the ice to rescue Pickles. Only Jordan did the right thing at the right time. He did a great job of explaining to the principal.*

Tom looked around at his friends. *It's nice to be a team. Together, maybe we can*

figure out how to do the right thing — at the right time, Tom thought. *Hockey rules!*

He couldn't wait for the next game.

*To Harty — for your love of the game,
as a player and a ref*
— I. P.

Contents

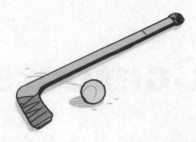

Road Hockey

Tom ran with the road hockey ball, stickhandling it toward the sidewalk. With a quick flick, he took a shot. Jordan caught it in his goalie glove.

"Sweet save!" said Jeff, flashing his crooked smile. Jeff was Tom's babysitter. He'd played hockey for ten years and knew everything about it.

Jordan gloated.

"Na, na! No goals on me!" He tossed the ball onto the street.

It rolled right to Stuart. Stuart slapped his stick and the ball dribbled into the net.

"Woo hoo! Great goal!" cheered Jeff, with a high-five.

Jordan made his scary goalie face and everyone laughed.

"Okay, road rats, time to shut the game down for tonight," said Jeff.

"What?" protested Tom. "Not yet!"

Jeff held up his hand. "'Fraid so. All of us have homework, right?"

"Homework? Yuck!" said Mark. "Road hockey is my kind of homework. It's practice for our next hockey game."

Tom, Mark, Stuart and Jordan played hockey for the Glenlake Hawks and they were supposed to practise as much as possible. "Yeah, Coach Howie's orders! Hockey homework," said Tom.

Jeff laughed. "Okay, okay. But only five more minutes." He unleashed a wrist shot.

Tom and his friends ran after the ball,

cheering, "Hockey rules! Yay, Jeff! Jeff's

the best!"

At 7:15 Jordan's watch beeped.

At 7:16 Stuart's mom phoned. "Get home!"

At 7:17 Mark's sister came by. "Home. Now!"

The game was officially over. Jordan shouldered his goalie pads. "Hey, Jeff, I want you to be my babysitter!" he said.

"Me, too!" said Stuart. "*Pleeeeease!*"

Jeff answered, "Sorry, Tom's mom has me totally booked up. Plus, I also . . ."

"Lucky Tom!" chimed his friends.

Yeah, thought Tom. *Jeff is the best and he's all mine.*

Rules Are Rules

The next night. Six o'clock.

Centennial Arena.

Coach Howie

blew his whistle and

motioned everyone in.

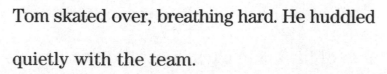

Tom skated over, breathing hard. He huddled

quietly with the team.

"Hawks, great drills tonight. You guys have been working hard and it's paying off!" said Coach Howie, clapping. "The Hockey Calgary website says we are rated number . . . ONE!"

"We're number one! We're number one!" Everyone cheered, banging their sticks on the ice. Tom liked Coach Howie. He liked his team. It felt great to be the best.

"Any questions tonight?" asked Coach Howie.

Tom wanted to ask about offside. Like lots of his teammates, he still didn't understand the rule about waiting for the puck to cross the blue line first.

"I've got a question," said Mark. "Should I get a hot dog or pickle chips after practice?"

Tom elbowed him.

Coach Howie rolled his eyes and cleared his throat. "Okay, then. Let's scrimmage for the last fifteen minutes. Split into two groups. Dark jerseys against light jerseys. Five on the ice, two on the bench."

Stuart, a defenceman, and Jordan, a goalie, wore dark jerseys. Tom waved for

Mark to stand with him. They both wore white jerseys.

The teams were ready. Coach Howie stood at centre ice. He dropped the puck. Tom won the faceoff, followed by a perfect pass to Mark.

Mark grabbed the puck and headed down the ice. Stuart followed, swiping at the puck. Mark lifted his stick for a slapshot. *WHUMPT!* It came down on Stuart's shoulder. Stuart lay on the ice like a starfish.

"Oooww-aaah," he groaned.

Coach Howie blew his whistle and the

game stopped. He crouched down beside Stuart. "You okay?"

Stuart's eyes were blank. "Yup." He stood slowly, with Mark's help. "Ooowwwhh . . ."

The team clapped their sticks on the ice.

Coach Howie's voice was firm. "Listen up. That was a high stick. You can't let this happen. You've got to control your stick! You could hit someone on the head. Give him a concussion. And it's a two-minute penalty — five minutes if there's an injury. Rules are rules."

Mark frowned. "I was only trying to score."

Coach Howie looked serious. "Everyone, watch this." He began to lift his stick. "Say stop when it's too high."

Up went his stick.

"STOP!" almost everyone yelled at the

same time, because almost everyone knew the high-sticking spot — above an opponent's shoulder.

"Okay, good! Now, NO high sticks!" Coach Howie dropped the puck for a faceoff.

A few minutes later, he stopped the game and reviewed the tripping penalty as Stuart rubbed his shins.

Tom rested on the bench with Mark.

"Remember when Coach Howie was more fun? He used to let us scrimmage without all these interruptions." Mark let out a giant breath. "Now it's start and stop and start and stop. We're just trying to score goals, right?"

Tom glanced at Coach Howie, about to blow his whistle again. "Hockey players who get lots of penalties are goons. I don't want to be a goon. Do you?"

Mark laughed. "Older players are goons, not us. They wipe players out on purpose. We're just trying to win. And to stay number one!" He rubbed his stomach. "I'm so hungry,

I could eat ten hot dogs and ten bags of pickle chips."

Suddenly, two light-jersey players flew to the bench. Tom and Mark quickly scrambled onto the ice into position. The puck slammed into Mark's stick. He passed the puck to Tom. Tom stickhandled it along the boards and behind the net. With a smooth turn, he did a perfect wraparound shot, and the puck slid by Jordan's goalie skate.

Coach Howie pointed at the net and smiled.

"Goal!" cheered Tom. "Yes!" He pumped

the air with his fist. "Yahoo!"

BANG! BANG! BANG! Tom looked
around. He could hear someone banging
on the spectator glass and shouting full
volume, "Yay, Tom! Great goal! You RULE!"

Jeff the Ref

At 6:15 the buzzer sounded. Practice was over.

Tom, Stuart, Mark and Jordan skated across the ice. When they got to the open gate, Jeff was waiting with a bag of chocolate caramels.

"Jeff!" yelped the boys, huddling around him.

"Great goal!" exclaimed Jeff. "Nice assist!" He slapped Tom and Mark high-fives.

Tom reached for a handful of candy. "Hey, what are you doing here?"

Jeff waved a small book. It was the same one he had been studying the other night — *Hockey Canada: Official Playing Rules*. There was a picture of a referee on the front cover. "I just passed the test. Now I'm a ref!"

"All right!" The boys whooped.

Jeff leaned toward them and whispered, "I'm a little nervous about being a ref, so you guys need to cheer me on."

They began to chant. "Jeff the Ref! Jeff the Ref! Jeff is the best!"

Jeff smiled. "Thanks, guys."

The four boys made their way to the dressing room, chanting faster and faster, "Jeff the Ref! Jeff the Ref! Jeff is the best!"

Tom swung open the door and announced to everyone, "My sitter is going to be the best ref in the world!"

"Yaaaaay, JEFF!" Mark screamed so loud, his mouthguard fell out.

Jordan looked at Tom enviously. "You're so lucky to have Jeff for your babysitter."

Tom smiled a lumpy chocolate caramel smile. He couldn't have agreed more.

City Helpers

Thursday. At school.

Tom, Mark, Stuart and Jordan sat at an art table drawing pictures of themselves for Social Studies as Mrs. Wong, their teacher, decorated a new bulletin board.

Stuart coloured a black eye on his picture. He was accident-prone and always had at least one bruise.

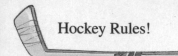

Jordan drew his scary goalie face.

"Here I am, wearing my Flames jersey," said Tom. "It used to be Jeff's."

"I'm going to give myself a moustache!" said Mark, looking for the brown marker.

Tom laughed. Mark always cracked him up.

"No way!" said Kylie, standing behind them. "Your portrait is supposed to be authentic. Like, *real*. Stop fooling around." She scooped up a handful of markers and went back to her table.

"Hey!" said Stuart. "Now there's no dark

red marker for scabs. And no beige for Band-Aids. How am I supposed to finish my picture?"

"Bring those markers back!" growled Jordan.

Kylie made a face.

"She should draw devil horns on hers," joked Mark.

Snop. Snop. Snop. Mrs. Wong stapled a map of Calgary onto the bulletin board. *Snop. Snop. Snop.* She stapled paper question marks around the map.

"Okay, people," said Mrs. Wong. "When

your portrait is cut out, staple it to the 'Our City' bulletin board. And now — I'd like you to think about our city and all the people who help to make it work. Who are our city helpers?"

Like an explosion, half the class

called out answers at the same time. "Doctor!" "Firefighter!" "Police officer!" "Hairdresser!" "Bus driver!" "Nurse!" Baker!"

"Excellent! Choose one that you'd like to know more about and draw that person. Their pictures will go on our bulletin board, too. Because . . . we are going to invite them to our classroom!" Mrs. Wong waved her hands in the air. "And even more exciting . . ."

She opened the cupboard behind her desk. Eight Monopoly games were stacked on the middle shelf. "You will get to play

Monopoly with our visitors — and ask them questions about our city."

"Yay!" everyone cheered.

Monopoly! Tom's eyes lit up. He loved Monopoly. He always played it with Grandma Dot. And he always won.

Amber Woznicki waved her hand. "You all know my dad, Officer Woz. He could be a visitor. And he's the best Monopoly player in the police department. I'm going to draw a picture of him in his police uniform."

"Hey, Tom," said Mark. "Wait till Officer Woz plays Monopoly with *you*! We'll see who's the best."

Tom said, "Right
on!" He could see
himself owning hotels
and houses on Boardwalk.

"I'm drawing a Zamboni driver," said
Mark to his group. "You gotta have good ice.
How do they work that machine, anyway?"

"I'm drawing the Flames goalie," said
Jordan.

"I can draw Coach Howie," said Stuart.
"With the water bottles."

"Hockey, hockey, hockey," said Kylie

with a groan. "How does *hockey* help our city?"

"Guess who I'm going to draw?" asked Tom. He tried to come up with somebody good. Fast.

"Who?" Kylie asked.

"A babysitter! Some parents can't work if they don't have one!" Tom flashed a toothy smile. He reached for a black marker and began to draw Jeff, wearing a black-and-white striped referee jersey.

"Good thinking!" Mrs. Wong nodded at Tom. "All people who work hard help to make our city better. It's a *team* effort." She held up some lined paper. "Your assignment, everyone, is to write down some amazing questions for our city helpers. Your good copies will go up on the board next to your pictures."

She wrote on the board:

OUR CITY Homework
— by Monday!

1. Finish your good copy of questions.

2. Read the Monopoly rules.

"Knowing the rules is important," said Mrs. Wong. "Playing by the rules makes the game fair for everyone. And I want lots of questions!"

Tom grinned. "Here's one: When's our next hockey game at Calgary Centennial Arena? And the answer is — Saturday. Two o'clock."

He and his friends all stuck two thumbs up.

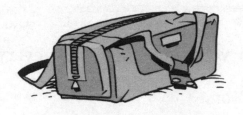

Game Time

Saturday. One o'clock.

"Everyone in the car!" hollered Dad.

"Okay," said Mom. She rushed around the house, turning off lights and grabbing her jacket, gloves and a blanket.

Tom and Mark loaded their hockey bags and sticks into the trunk.

"Are you sure you've got everything?" asked Mom.

"Yup." Tom nodded. "But we need to pick up Jordan."

They pulled up in front of Jordan's house. Mom honked. Several minutes later, Jordan stumbled out the door, lugging his huge goalie bag. Tom wished he had the

courage to tell him to stop being late.

Jordan stuffed his bag and stick into the trunk. "Homework," he growled. "My mom made me start on those questions! I hate writing." He lowered his voice. "So far, I just used Kylie's: How does hockey help our city?"

"Did I hear homework?" asked Mom.

"We have to write questions about our city," said Tom.

"Like . . . ?" asked Mom.

"Who delivers mail to the Calgary Flames?" joked Mark.

"A firefighter!" chuckled Dad.

"Wow, you got it! Flames!"

Everyone laughed.

"Here's another question. What team do we play?" asked Mark.

"Brentwood Bears," said Jordan.

"Oh, no, Brentwood Bears! Those guys are BIG!" said Tom. "They've got that giant guy on defence! He wears men's shoulder pads and he's way taller than me."

"They freak me out," said Mark.

"The Bears should be going after the puck, not the players," said Mom.

"Maybe Jeff will be your ref!" added Dad.

"Yeah!" said Tom. "Jeff the Ref. Jeff is the best! He'll protect us!"

"Well — a ref is there to protect the rules," said Mom.

The boys rolled their eyes.

The car finally turned off busy Crowchild Trail and headed toward the arena. Tom looked at the clock on the dashboard. His stomach twisted. "Step on the gas, Mom. We're going to be late!"

She slowed down.

"Mom! Pleeeeease go faster!"

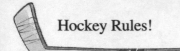

"Sorry, guys." Mom pointed to the playground. "I'll get a speeding ticket."

Tom scrunched his forehead. "Here's a question for Officer Woz: Why do we have to go slow here when it makes us late for hockey?"

Jeff Is the Best

They hurried through the arena doors and down the hall to their dressing room. Everyone inside was ready for the game.

"Where were you guys?" asked Stuart.

"I was getting worried," said Coach Howie. "Remember — the rule is to be here half an hour before game time."

Tom hated being late. He watched the

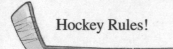

rest of his team file out the door.

Mark didn't look up. He was searching through his bag for something.

— ● —

Both teams were into their warm-ups.

The Hawks skated fast backward, in a tight circle. Tom launched onto the ice. He kept his eyes down as he broke into the line of skaters. When he lifted his head, he saw — Jeff!

Jeff was wearing black pants, a black-and-white striped referee jersey and a special helmet with a clear visor. He had a

shiny whistle wrapped around his knuckles and his ref's rule book poked out of his back pocket.

"Hey, Jeff!" called Tom.

Jeff looked over and gave him a weird half wave.

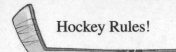

"Where's the linesman?" Tom asked Coach Howie.

"We just have one ref today," he said. "He'll be busy."

BUZZZZZ. The time clock sounded.

The team huddled around Jordan. They yelled *"HAWKS!"* and then took their positions.

Jeff stood at centre ice. Tom tried to stay cool, but excitement bubbled inside. *Jeff the Ref! Jeff the Ref! Jeff is the BEST!* He had always wished he could play on the same team as Jeff. This was the next best thing.

Jeff leaned forward. He blew his whistle. With a shaky *plop* the puck dropped. Not the best. It bounced — then rolled like a doughnut on the loose.

Tom flicked his stick and the puck went right to the Bears' centre. The Bear flew down the ice. Jeff followed, his eyes glued to the action.

Tom dug in his blades and bolted after the puck. He reached out his stick.

THWACK! Tom felt his legs disappear. He hit the ice.

Jeff's hand went up. His whistle blew. He

signalled tripping on the Bear who nailed Tom.

Tom shook himself as he stood. Wincing, he rubbed his wrist. "Oooooh," he moaned softly. He heard Jeff make the call at the scorekeeper's window: "Number 16 Bears — two minutes for tripping."

For a second Tom's wince became a smile. Jeff was an awesome ref. Probably the best ref ever — if you didn't count the puck drop.

— ● —

The Hawks were now on a power play with only four Bears on the ice. Tom stood in the players' box. His wrist throbbed.

"These guys are huge!" said Stuart.

Tom tried not to think about the size of the Bears. When he'd faced off with their giant centre, he had tried not to look at him. *Stay brave*, Tom told himself. *We're the best! We RULE!* He looked at Mark. "This is our big chance to score. We're five on four."

They got ready to step onto the ice.

"Keep your heads up," said Coach Howie.

Tom rushed into the action.

The Bears didn't let up. They skated in front of the Hawks net, trying to block Jordan's view. Jordan went into a crouch. A Bear blasted a backhand wrist shot. Jordan deflected the puck. Another Bear took a shot.

WHOMP! The puck slid through Jordan's legs and into the net.

Tom's heart sank. How did the Bears score short-handed?

WHEEEEE! Jeff blew his whistle. But he did not point at the net. He crossed his arms in front of his chest, then swept them outward.

"What . . .?" Tom nudged Mark.

"No goal!" announced Jeff. "Net was off!"

"Ohhhhhhhhh!" wailed the players on the

Bears bench. They shook their sticks and

stomped their skates. Wearing black jerseys

and helmets, they looked like angry, real black bears.

"Woo HOO!" cheered the Hawks, as Jeff set their net in proper position.

Coach Howie said, "Keep the cheering

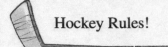

down. A ref can give us a bench penalty."

"Not Jeff!" said Tom. "He's our friend."

Coach Howie's face went red. "Right now, Tom, Jeff is the ref first and your friend second."

Hawks vs. Bears

Second period. The score was 0–0.

"Go, Hawks, go!" cheered the spectators from the stands.

But no matter how hard and fast they played, the Hawks couldn't score.

"Keep trying," said Coach Howie. "Go full out."

Tom tried to think about shooting and scoring — and skating fast. The problem was, the fast skating was making him tired. And the Bears seemed to be getting bigger and stronger — and faster!

—●—

It was now the third period. The score was still 0–0. "Go, Hawks, go!" yelled the Hawks bench. The puck flew end to end. Up and down the ice it passed, from one player to the next.

Finally Tom had the puck. The biggest Bear defenceman charged forward. Tom

deked around him. *BAM!* The Bear knocked
Jeff over and fell on top of him, sending
them spinning round and round. *WHEEEE!*
Jeff blew his whistle and at the same instant,
Tom unleashed his wicked slapshot. Ping!
The puck flew right into the net.

"Goal!" exclaimed Tom. A rush of excitement bolted through him. "Yes! Yes! Yes!" He pumped the air with his fist.

"Yahoo!" cheered the Hawks.

"YAY!" cheered the fans.

But Jeff signalled no goal.

"No goal?" gasped the Hawks.

Jeff skated over, brushing the frost off his pants. "I lost sight of the puck when the Bears player fell on top of me," he explained. "I had to blow the whistle."

"That was a beautiful goal," said Stuart, punching Tom's shoulder. "I saw it." Tom skated toward the bench, deflated. *How in the world could Jeff miss my wicked slapshot — and the goal?*

— ● —

The clock was running out of time.

"Let's go, Hawks, let's go!" hollered the fans.

Mark had the puck. He skated neck and neck with a Bear toward the blue line. As he raised his stick to pass — *WHAM!* The Bear fell.

Jeff's whistle blew.

Again? thought Tom. Then he saw Jeff's call.

"High stick."
Jeff pointed to
Mark. "And —
offside!" Jeff
pointed to Tom.

Tom checked his feet. He was on
the wrong side of the blue line. *This is
so unfair! It's like the Hawks can't do
anything right.*

Jeff skated Mark over to the penalty box.

"I was only trying to pass," said Mark.

Jeff stopped. He looked at Mark. "Where
is your mouthguard?" he asked. "Once

your penalty's up, you can't go back on the ice without one."

"Huh?" said Mark. "But I couldn't find it!"

"I think it fell out when you cheered for Jeff at practice," said Stuart.

"You're off the ice as of right now," said Jeff. "Minor Hockey rule."

Mark plopped down on the bench. "Guys, can I borrow a mouthguard?"

"YUCK!" everyone screamed.

Jeff skated into position and dropped the puck at the faceoff dot.

The Bears won the faceoff and began

charging down the ice. Then Stuart, skating

backwards, tripped over his feet, leaving

the Bears with a three-on-one.

"Oh, no!" gasped Tom. He tried to catch

up to the rush.

Tic-tac-toe. *SWOOSH!* The puck sat in

the back of the net, following the Bears' perfect passing play and goal.

"YAY!" screamed the Bears, banging their sticks.

Jordan dug out the puck. Tom couldn't believe his eyes.

Jeff Is the Worst

The final score was 1–0 — for the Bears.

As Tom filed into line to shake hands, he saw Jeff skate slowly off the ice. Anger burned inside him. *Why had Jeff been so mean to the Hawks?*

Comments swirled around Tom as the team headed for the dressing room.

"Your goal should have counted."

"We were robbed — big time."

"Jeff was the *worst*!"

"He called everything! Even two at a time! That's . . ."

"Unreal!"

"Unbelievable!"

In the noisy dressing room Tom sat holding a small bag of ice on his throbbing wrist. He peeked under the bag. His skin was turning blue.

Coach Howie blew his whistle. "We've got a lot of work to do next practice." He

waved the game sheet in the air and pointed to the list of penalties. "We played short-handed for eight minutes due to penalties. We made mistakes. And it killed us. We are better than that. Remember what I said at the last practice: use skills, not tricks. Do your best. And wear your mouthguard." He looked directly at Mark, then at Tom and Jordan, too. "And — don't be late!"

Everyone took a deep breath. They all

knew the Hawks were better than that. And it didn't feel good to be reminded.

Coach Howie walked over to Tom. "How's the wrist?"

Tom's eyes were wet. "Okay," he answered. But he could feel it swelling up like a jumbo sausage.

"Good," said Coach Howie. "That was a bad trip you got from that Bear. You're lucky it's not broken." He sighed. "I hate to see any player hurt. Doesn't matter what team they're on. That's what ended all my hopes of playing for the NHL. I got smashed into the boards and wrecked my knee. Nobody in the NHL wants a hockey player with a bad knee. Or a bad wrist."

Tom gulped. He always dreamed of playing for the NHL!

Jordan looked at Tom. "That Bear should have gotten five minutes for hurting you. And he should've been kicked out!"

"Here, this fell out of Jeff's pocket," Coach Howie said. He passed Tom Jeff's book, *Hockey Canada: Official Playing Rules*. "Please give it to him the next time you see him."

Tom shoved the book to the bottom of
his bag — next to his smelly socks.

Dead Ducks

Sunday.

Knock, knock, knock. When Tom opened his front door, Jordan, Mark and Stuart were there, ready to play road hockey.

"Homework first!" hollered Mom from the kitchen. "Have you written up those questions? And gone over the Monopoly rules?"

Mark frowned. "I've got a new question:

Why did Jeff call high sticking on me? I was just trying to pass the puck. And that Bears guy was way bigger!"

"Jeff stunk," said Jordan.

"He killed us with penalties!" said Stuart, shaking his head.

Tom grimaced. "He missed my perfect goal!"

"Some *friend*!" they agreed.

"Let's check out our team stats on the computer," Tom said. His friends left their boots at the door and followed him to his mom's office. He clicked on the internet

symbol and scrolled down to the website

for Hockey Calgary. "Here we are!" The

boys huddled around the screen.

"We're tied for second!" said Stuart.

"What happened? We were first!"

"Who are we tied with?" asked Jordan.

"Um . . ." Tom followed the chart. "The Bears."

"See?" snapped Mark. "We should have won that game and we'd still be first! The Bears were behind us!"

Tom's mom called from the kitchen, "While you're on the computer, Tom, please send Jeff a reminder about babysitting on Monday."

Tom pulled up his mom's email program and found Jeff's address.

"Wow!" said Jordan. "You're good at this."

"Let me see," said Stuart.

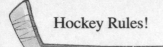

Tom started the message.

Dear Jeff,

With a funny smile on his face, he typed:

We were robbed! My goal should have counted.

Mark laughed. "Yeah. ROBBED! It was a stickup. Get it? A hockey stick up! Hey, let me write some." He pushed Tom away from the keyboard.

I didn't really high stick. And mouthguards make me gag. And they could give you buckteeth.

Everyone snickered.

"No more penalties! No more penalties!"

they chanted.

Then Jordan added:

> **You stink. Sorry. We don't like stinkers.**

Stuart finished off with:

> **From the guys you used to be nice to:**

> **Tom, Stuart, Jordan and Mark**

He inserted four unhappy faces:

They were all laughing. Tom read the

whole email as his friends chanted, "No

more penalties! No more penalties! Jeff is the worst! Jeff is the worst!" over and over.

A cool shiver went up Tom's back. "Whoa, whoa!" he said. "We gotta delete this and email him about the babysitting. Besides, we don't hate *him* — we just hate some of the rules. That picky I-can't-see-the-puck rule cost us the game."

Tom moved the mouse to delete the message. He clicked. "Oh, no!" he gasped. "I think I screwed up."

The screen said: Sending. A picture of

an envelope flew across the bottom of the email.

Everyone spoke at the same time. "I was joking." "What happened?" "We didn't mean it." "Why did your mom tell us to email anyway?"

"Quick!" Tom panicked. "We have to send him another one." He wrote:

> **Please please please ignore the last email. It was a bad bad joke.**

He pressed the Send symbol again. He stared at the blank computer screen and then at his friends. They all looked guilty. Tom felt horrible. His stomach spun the way it did at hockey tryouts. "Do you think the first email really went to Jeff?"

"We don't have email, so I don't know," said Jordan.

"Jeff can take a joke, right?" asked Mark.

"We were just kidding," added Stuart.

Tom sighed. "What should we do now?"

"I gotta get home," said Jordan.

The others nodded.

"Hey, Hawks — we're dead ducks," mumbled Mark, jamming on his boots.

— ● —

Tom felt sick. He crawled into bed, zapped. His thoughts were jumbled up like a wad of old hockey tape covered in sock lint. He was mad Mark hadn't worn his mouthguard. He was glad the Bear got a penalty for tripping him. He was glad the Bears' first goal was called off. He was mad his own goal was called off. He wished he'd asked Coach Howie to explain offside again. He wished he hadn't pressed Send by mistake.

Tom thought about Jeff. *Why did I tell him we were robbed? Why did Jordan say he stunk?*

Jeff usually babysat Monday. And that was tomorrow.

Tom began to sweat.

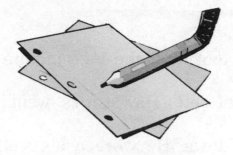

Classroom Rules

Monday afternoon after recess.

Mrs. Wong stood beside the "Our City" bulletin board, looking at the drawings. "Wonderful. Wonderful. We have a firefighter . . . the Flames goalie . . . a nurse . . . Officer Woz . . . a Zamboni operator . . . a carpenter . . . a hairdresser . . . a referee . . ."

Tom looked at the nice picture he had drawn of Jeff. The stripes went straight up and down. He wore a big smile. Tom wondered if Jeff was smiling today.

"Now for the final copies of your questions," said Mrs. Wong. "Let's see. Jordan has a question beside his Flames goalie picture." She read: "How can hockey help our city?" Mrs. Wong smiled. "Good question, Jordan." She scrunched up her forehead. "I want to answer this one! I think hockey gives Calgary more city spirit. I own a Flames jersey and I have a flag on my car!"

"Go, Flames, go!" cheered some of the kids.

Mrs. Wong is right, thought Tom. *Hockey spirit is fun*. But he didn't feel the spirit right now. Right now he felt pukey.

"Oh, my!" exclaimed Mrs. Wong, looking at the biggest picture on the bulletin board. "That looks like me!"

Kylie said, "It *is*! With diamond earrings! Read my first question, Mrs. Wong."

"Okay, it's: How do you decide what rules to make for the class?" Mrs. Wong thought for a moment. "Well, my rules are all about safety, respect and schoolwork. I always try to be fair. Rules make things fair for everyone." She clapped and sang out, "I stay cool with classroom rules!"

Tom smiled. He liked Mrs. Wong.

She looked at her watch. "Okay, people, *if* you have your questions on our bulletin board, and *if* you've read the Monopoly rules, you can play Monopoly till the bell rings."

"Amber! Jill!" said Kylie. "C'mon, let's take the purple table!"

"Woo-eee, Monopoly!" Everyone headed for the games. Everyone except Tom. He looked at his blank page and let out a big sigh. He knew it was fair. Mrs. Wong was just enforcing her finish-your-homework-first rule.

Tom sat at his desk listening to the other kids play Monopoly.

"I'm buying Boardwalk." "I got Free Parking!" "Roll the dice." "Go directly to Jail."

"That'll be 50 bucks." "Your turn."

He tried to think up some good city helper questions for his picture of Jeff. *Should they be about babysitting? Or should they be about reffing?* His mind was frozen on one thing — the email.

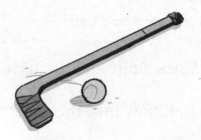

Winning Isn't Everything

At four o'clock, the boys were at Tom's house, playing road hockey. Stuart and Mark were teamed against Tom, trying to score on Jordan. The score was 3–0 for Stuart and Mark.

Stuart had the ball. He quickly passed

to Mark. Mark unleashed a hard slapshot. Bam! The ball flew into the net.

"Yes!" raved Stuart. "We got another one!"

Tom needed help, playing against two. Where was Jeff?

Jordan tossed the ball down the street.

Tom sprinted after it. *Go, go, go,* he told himself. His feet were on fire. Stuart and Mark caught up to him. Tom turned, hugging the ball with his stick. Mark snatched it away — again.

Tom sighed, frustrated. Two against one

was a rip-off. How could he win? He didn't have a chance.

Mark passed the ball to Stuart. Stuart easily passed it back to Mark. Suddenly Tom jabbed just a bit of his stick between Mark's legs.

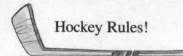

"*Aaiii!*" shrieked Mark. He wiped out.

Tom got hold of the ball and fired a blazing shot. *SMACK!* It hit the crossbar, sliding the net across the pavement. Jordan centred the net while Stuart ran down the street, chasing the loose, bouncing ball.

Mark picked himself up and brushed off the snow. His jeans had a big hole at the knee.

Tom banged his stick. "No goal, again!"

Mark pointed at him. "Hey, you tripped me! That's a dirty move — just because you want to score!"

"Me, dirty? You get more penalties than anyone on the team!" blurted Tom. "Remember, the Bears scored when you had a penalty!"

Mark glared.

"Come on, guys! Quit fighting!" said Stuart. "Winning isn't everything!"

Tom looked at Mark's ripped knee. And tripping wasn't fair. "Sorry."

"Okay, let's go!" Stuart shot the ball back into play to Mark. When Mark turned, Tom was there. He lifted the ball off Mark's stick and ran with it. Jordan crouched in net. Tom circled wide, then flicked the ball back. It flew into the net.

"Goal!" cheered Tom, pumping his fist in the air. "Finally!"

"What a shot!" said Jordan.

"Awesome!" howled Stuart.

"Yeah," said Mark, punching Tom's shoulder. "You rule!"

Stuart held his fist out and the boys banged their fists on top. "Road rats!"

Tom looked down the street. Where was Jeff?

Time Out

A car was slowly creeping toward them.

"Hey, it's my Grandma Dot!" Tom waved.

What is she doing here? he wondered.

Grandma Dot parked her car and got out,

holding a large cookie tin. "Hello, boys," she

said. "How about a time out?" She took off

the lid and each of them happily gobbled

down a soft cookie loaded with chocolate

chips. "That was some hockey game you boys played the other day."

Jordan growled, "We lost."

"I saw that," said Grandma Dot.

"We were really mad," said Tom. "We got all these penalties called on us."

"Well, I got one too — a parking ticket. Rules are rules! Now, come on in, Tom. It's too cold to be playing on the street. And it's dangerous!"

Jordan nudged Stuart. Stuart nudged Mark. When Jeff babysat, they always played on the street, even when it was snowing.

Tom whispered to his friends, "Come back after dinner. We'll play road hockey, eat more cookies and maybe Jeff will be here."

Grandma Dot said, "After dinner, Tom has a few things to do — including homework, I'm sure." She smiled.

"What about Jeff?" asked Stuart.

Grandma Dot picked up the ball and put it in her bag. "I'm the babysitter." She walked toward the house and opened the front door. "Say goodbye to your friends, Tom."

But what about Jeff? Tom's stomach flipped.

"Do you think he quit?" asked Jordan.

"Inside, right now!" hollered Grandma Dot.

Jeff quit? Tom felt like he'd been body-checked. He wanted to cry — just like he did the time he was bodychecked into the boards.

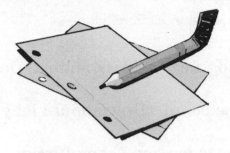

Shared Respect

Tom put his hockey gloves and boots in the mudroom. A puck-sized lump was stuck in his throat.

"What first — a shower or your homework?" asked Grandma Dot.

"Well-l-l-l . . ." said Tom, "part of my homework is Monopoly . . ."

"Wonderful!" said Grandma Dot. They set up the board. "How about I let you have two turns to my one," she offered. "And you can skip going to Jail. And you can collect five hundred dollars when you pass Go!"

"Grandma!" said Tom. "It'll be too easy!"

"Don't you like to win?" She winked.

Tom thought about it. *I do love winning. It always feels better than losing. But — did she let me win? All those times?* A little light bulb went on in his brain. "You mean I'm *not* the best Monopoly player?" He looked right into Grandma Dot's eyes.

"Well, maybe I gave you just a bit of an advantage once or twice," she admitted.

"Oh, boy. Oh, man. Well, no more!" said Tom. "I have to play by the rules. All the rules. Because next week I might get to play Officer Woz. And it's got to be a fair game!"

Grandma Dot smiled. "Okay, Tom, you asked for it! No more half-price properties!" She handed Tom the Monopoly rules.

Tom began to read.

"From now on, look out," said Grandma Dot, "because I'm really good at this game. And I'm going to be a stickler for the rules."

"You're on!" said Tom. He wondered if he would ever beat her at Monopoly again. *Gee, it's kind of fun to think I'll have to try my best, play by all the rules and not be so sure I'll win.*

Then Grandma Dot's cellphone rang and she went to the hall to talk.

Tom had an idea. I could work on my other homework. He grabbed his backpack and sat at the kitchen table.

He tapped his hockey pencil, thinking about questions and Jeff.

Finally, he wrote:

Dear Jeff,
It's not good to tell a ref he stinks.

"Nope!" Tom scrunched up the paper.

He started again.

Dear Jeff,
It's good for a ref to be a stickler.
Get it? Hockey stick — tickler.

"Nope!" Tom scrunched up the paper.

He started again.

Dear Jeff,
Sorry again about the email. Will you
please be my babysitter? We like you
very very very much.

Tom pressed so hard on his pencil that it snapped in half. He looked for some tape in the drawer. When he couldn't find any, he went to his hockey bag for his sock tape. It was stuck to Jeff's little book, *Hockey Canada: Official Playing Rules.*

On the cover, there was a picture of a ref and a message. It said: "Shared Respect. Players. Coaches. Officials. Parents." Tom opened it. On page twelve, there was a message from Hockey Canada: "A game should be refereed strictly in accordance with the rules."

Every rule was there in black and white — with pictures. Every rule was clearly spelled out by Hockey Canada — every rule the Hawks had broken. Jeff was only trying to be the best ref.

Tom wrapped a piece of sock tape around his pencil. He held onto the wiggly part and wrote,

Being a ref must be hard. You have to skate really fast. And know when to blow your whistle. You have to remember all the rules — even the ones nobody likes. Mrs. Wong said a teacher makes rules to be fair. You

showed me that a ref has to follow

the hockey rules, no matter what.

Too bad if his friends don't like it.

From your friend, Tom

PS: Winning isn't everything.

PPS: You can eat all the cookies.

PPPS: You don't really stink.

PPPS: Please STICK with me. Get it?

Hockey stick!

At the bottom, Tom

drew a ref jersey

with his black

marker. Then he

folded the letter

and put it in Grandma Dot's cookie tin. Maybe she would drive him to Jeff's house if he asked. He could leave the tin on Jeff's steps.

Tom sighed. He wished he'd stopped himself and his friends from writing the bad stuff. He closed his eyes and imagined a giant ref's whistle. *WHEEEEE! STOP!* Suddenly, Tom thought of a great question for Jeff for the class project: *How would hockey games be different if there weren't any rules?*

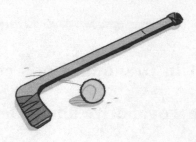

Hockey Rules!

Grandma Dot came into the kitchen.

"Oh dear," she said, looking out the window and buttoning her coat. "It's snowing." She patted Tom on the shoulder. "I'd better get home before the roads get bad."

"You're leaving?" said Tom.

"Jeff's here now. He'll babysit till your

mom and dad get home," said Grandma Dot, opening the door. "I was only a *call-up* till he got here." She waved goodbye. "See you at your game. Go, Hawks, go!"

Jeff stepped inside. His hair was wet and his cheeks were glowing red.

Tom's face turned red. He couldn't think of anything to say. He went to get the cookie tin.

Jeff read the letter a couple of times. He ate a couple of cookies.

Tom gulped back a sick feeling. *What is he thinking?* he wondered.

Finally, Jeff said, "I've been playing hockey for years. I didn't always like the refs' calls either. I got suspended three times. Once I broke my arm. Then I figured it out. When I played my best — *and* played by the rules — there was nothing better." Jeff stuffed another cookie into his mouth. "And now I know how hard it is to be a ref."

Tom breathed a sigh of relief. *Phew.* Jeff wasn't too mad after all. He was so cool.

"Maybe one day you'll be a ref and you'll find out!" Jeff ruffled Tom's hair.

Tom smiled. He'd like to be a ref one day. He was glad he'd chosen Jeff the Ref for the city project.

Jeff reached into his duffle bag. He pulled out a bag of four green blobby things. "Mouthguards. They were giving them away free at the refs' clinic," he said. "Give one to Mark, okay? You know you guys gotta wear them to prevent injuries. And penalties!" He winked.

"Thanks!" Tom smiled. "Can I phone him and tell him?"

"Sure!" Jeff smiled back. "Invite him over. And Stuart and Jordan. Let's play road hockey!" He downed two more cookies.

"Woo hoo!" yelped Tom. "And we're playing full rules now." He grabbed his Flames jersey and pulled it over his head.

"You're on!" Jeff opened the front door.

Snow fluttered down in the light from the street lamp. As they got the net from the garage, Tom asked, "Do you think, if you got invited, you'd be able to visit my classroom?"

——●——

When Stuart, Mark and Jordan arrived, they approached Jeff shyly.

Stuart spoke for them. "We're sorry for the email." All three faces were serious.

"Here. These are for you." Mark held out a bag of pickle chips. "I'm really going to watch raising my stick."

Jeff flashed his crooked smile. "Hockey rules! Shared respect!"

As Jordan buckled his goalie pads, Jeff said, "Okay, men — Tom says it's full rules from now on, so I have to teach you one more . . ." His face turned mischievous. "When the Flames are in the playoffs — NO shaving! It's bad luck!"

Everyone cracked up.

Tom reached into his pocket and pulled out his black marker. He scribbled a crooked line above his upper lip. "Who else wants a moustache?"

"Me! Me!" said Mark. "A big droopy one!"

"Give me a beard," said Stuart.

"Beard and moustache for me," snorted Jordan.

"Goatee, right here," said Jeff, pointing to his chin.

When they were done they looked at each other and fell back on the snowbank, laughing.

Jeff held up the road hockey ball. "Okay road-rat dudes, I'm ready! It's hockey time!"

He dropped the ball and passed it to Tom.

Tom took a shot. "Yahoo!" he shouted. "Game on!"

Jeff really is the best sitter in the world, he thought. *And the best ref.*

Irene Punt Meets the Stanley Cup

My family spends every summer in Whitefish, Montana, hanging out at our lake house, located on Whitefish Lake.

The summer of 2011 was very COOL. Our friend and neighbour, Doug Houda, was the assistant coach of the Boston Bruins and they had just won the Stanley Cup!

Every year the NHL gives each member of the winning team one day to spend with the big silver trophy. Lucky for us, Doug wanted his "day with the Stanley Cup" to be in Whitefish.

The Stanley Cup arrived by private jet at the Kalispell airport. It was accompanied by the "Keeper of the Cup" who is a representative of the Hockey Hall of Fame. The "Keeper" looks after the Cup every day. He makes sure the Cup stays safe and stays on its visiting schedule.

The Cup travelled from the airport to Doug's house, where it was loaded onto a pontoon boat. Soon, it started its journey down the lake, in the direction of a party being held in its honour. A line of boats followed the pontoon boat, like a floating parade.

My hockey-loving family and I waited anxiously on our dock with cameras ready. Soon, the boat was in view and we could see the shiny silver Cup heading our way. The excitement was huge! "Yay!" we cheered, as the boat came to a stop at the end of our dock.

Amazing! We were able to touch the Cup, kiss the Cup and read the names of all who have won it. Then the pontoon boat continued down the lake and we joined the parade.

When we pulled our boat up to the party dock, another boat was unloading a bunch of kids, all jumping with joy. I looked at them and said "You guys look really excited to party with the Stanley Cup. So am I!"

Then one of the moms said to me, "No, Irene. They are more excited to see you — because you write their favourite hockey books!"

WOW! The summer of 2011 was extra cool — thanks to the Stanley Cup, my readers and hockey, of course!

Keep your stick on the ice and KEEP READING!

— *Irene Punt*

Read more of Irene Punt's Glenlake Hawks books!

The Rink Rats

The local outdoor rink needs a lot of work. Tom and his friends pledge to perfect it in time for the annual Family Day hockey game and soon get to it. But it's more work than the boys thought . . . and even worse, the Hawks are losing! Can they come up with a game plan?

978-1-4431-0442-5

Tryout Trouble

Tom is so happy when Harty, the boy he met at hockey camp in *The Wicked Slapshot*, moves into the neighbourhood! That is, until Tom realizes that Harty will be competing with him for a spot on the Hawks — and he seems to be winning over all of Tom's teammates!

978-1-4431-3345-6

Hockey Luck

It's a new season and everyone but Tom has a good luck charm. Mark eats pizza before a game; Harty dresses in a certain order; Stuart wears NHL Band-Aids and Jordan never washes his socks. But Tom's new number is proving to be a unlucky. How can he turn his luck around?

978-1-4431-4278-6